*"I'm one of them now."*

They turned quickly to look behind them. A bandit was standing at the rail. He held a crossbow on Len and Miles. When the bandit moved closer, Miles recognized him.

"Vinnie!"

Vinnie waved the crossbow at them. "I'm one of them now. You can call me Razorback. I joined up with Meat Hook. He trusts me now. He sent me here to look around."

Collect *ESCAPE FROM LOST ISLAND*
Available from HarperPaperbacks

#1  Stranded!
#2  Attack!
#3  Mutiny!
#4  Discovered!
#5  Revenge!
#6  Escape!

# Mutiny!

## Clay Coleman

# HarperPaperbacks
*A Division of* HarperCollins*Publishers*

*For Peter Holt Calderwood*

This is a work of fiction. The characters, incidents, and dialogues are products of the author's imagination and are not to be construed as real. Any resemblance to actual events or persons, living or dead, is entirely coincidental.

HarperPaperbacks  *A Division of* HarperCollins*Publishers*
10 East 53rd Street, New York, N.Y. 10022

Produced by Daniel Weiss Associates, Inc.
33 West 17th Street, New York, New York 10011.

RL 4.8   IL 008–012
First printing: January, 1991

Printed in the United States of America

HarperPaperbacks and colophon are trademarks of HarperCollins*Publishers*

10  9  8  7  6  5  4  3  2  1

# Mutiny!

# One

"No!" Len cried. "Don't die, Miles! Please don't die."

Len Hayden hovered over the pale figure of his friend Miles Bookman. Miles lay bleeding in the white sand of the beach on Apocalypse Island. An aluminum arrow protruded from his stomach. The arrow had come from the crossbow of Dog Face, one of the hideous mutants from Lost Island, to the south.

Cruiser, a skinny, long-haired kid, leaned over and looked at Miles. "He's not dead. He just passed out. Look—he's still breathing."

"He *is* alive!" Len said. "Thank God!"

Cruiser drew back, peering toward the dense green jungle above them. He had never been up to the laboratory where the secret experiments had taken place. The experiments had produced Dog Face and the rest of the bandit warriors who had then fled to Lost Island. A plane wreck

1

a few weeks ago had left the boys in the realm of the warriors, though the kids had managed to fight back and stay alive on Apocalypse Island.

Len looked back over his shoulder, staring toward the jungle. "We've got to take Miles to the lab. He's going to die if we don't help him. Augie, D.J.—give me a hand here."

The two smaller boys were frowning at Miles. Augie stood next to a large wolflike dog that he had found, befriended, and named Commando. The dog had once been part of the experiments on the island. D.J. wore a punky haircut and the remains of a tattered sweatshirt. Both of them had been frightened by the horrors of the night before and this morning.

"Is he really alive?" D.J. asked.

Len nodded frantically. "We've got to carry him to the lab and get this arrow out of him."

Augie knelt beside the fallen boy. "He can't die, Hayden. I like Miles. He was good to me."

Miles stirred and opened his eyes to look up at Len. "Hayden," he said weakly. "It hurts."

"Hang on," Len replied. "You'll be all right, Miles. We'll take care of you as soon as we get you to the lab."

"The hangar," Miles said. "Go there—you—"

Miles lost strength and closed his eyes again. Sweat beaded on his ashen face, and a shiver ran through his wounded body.

Len started to lift Miles's shoulder. "D.J., you

and Augie get his feet. Come on—we've got to hurry."

D.J. shook his head. "No way. I'm not touching him. He looks creepy."

Len gawked at the younger boy. "Get real, D.J. He'll die without us. You can't let him die, can you?"

Cruiser stepped in front of D.J. "He doesn't have to touch him. The prep is history anyway. We've got to take this boat and get out of here before those mutants come after us."

Len scowled at Cruiser. "You'd leave him! That's just like you juvenile delinquents. You can't think about anyone but yourselves."

"Better than preppie scum like you," Cruiser replied with a hostile glare. "Your friend is dead meat. Face it."

Len stood up. "We could have left you on Lost Island last night, Cruiser. But we didn't. Miles and I came back for you."

Cruiser shuddered, unable to speak. Images of the rescue attempt were still fresh in his mind. The night before, they had tried to rescue two of the others who were stuck in the bandit camp on Lost Island, but they had failed. Cruiser still couldn't believe what he had seen. Vinnie and Joey had actually been locked up in hanging cages, prisoners of the mutant forces.

Len looked down at Miles again. "We've got to get him up to the lab. It's our only chance."

Augie started to grab Miles's legs, but Cruiser suddenly pushed Augie into the sand. Commando growled and tensed.

"No!" Augie cried. "No, Commando!"

The dog stopped cold. Its eyes were fixed on Cruiser. Commando was loyal to Augie and would attack anyone who tried to hurt the boy.

Cruiser's eyes grew wide. "Keep that beast off me."

Augie jumped to his feet and stood beside the dog. "You aren't the boss, Cruiser. Don't tell me what to do."

D.J. whimpered, "I'm afraid."

"Shut up," Cruiser said. "You're acting like a wimp."

Len couldn't believe that the others were refusing to help. "We've got to get him to the lab. He'll die if we don't. We can't let him die."

"You shut up, too," Cruiser snapped.

Len pointed a finger at him. "I'm not afraid of you!"

Cruiser jumped straight at Len and knocked him to the sand. They began to wrestle on the beach.

As they fought, a broad shadow fell over them and two large hands reached down to grab their shoulders. Neil Kirkland, a tall, muscular, dark-haired boy of sixteen, lifted them from the sand. He had been chasing the mutant who had fired

4

the crossbow at Miles. Kirkland held Cruiser and Len at arm's length.

"Look at you," Kirkland said. "I lose that bandit and come back here to find you doing the main event."

Kirkland pushed them in opposite directions. "Chill out! We've got enough trouble."

Len pointed toward his wounded friend. "We've got to take Miles to the lab, Kirkland. He's going to die if we don't help him."

Kirkland's face went slack. He stared down at the still figure of Miles Bookman. Kirkland had seen a dead man once, and the resemblance was close.

"He's in bad shape, all right," the older boy said.

Cruiser leaned closer to Kirkland. "He's gone. We've got to take the boat and clear out while we're still alive."

Kirkland turned to the south and gazed in the direction of Lost Island. He wondered how long it would take before Meat Hook and Bullet Head rallied the mutant fleet. The attack of the castaways had disrupted Meat Hook's camp, but the boys hadn't been able to do any real damage. They hadn't been able to rescue Vinnie and Joey, the two other boys who had gone down in the plane wreck with them.

Waves lapped harmlessly against the white sand of the beach. If not for the threat from the

5

mutant camp, it would have been a perfect tropical morning.

Under his breath, Kirkland cursed the storm that had left them stranded on this island in the South Seas. He looked at Miles again. Kirkland didn't consider Miles his friend, but the kid had brains and guts.

Kirkland couldn't let him die. Miles had saved Kirkland's life, so Kirkland owed him. He had to square the debt.

Kirkland nodded. "Okay. We'll take him to the lab."

Len grabbed Miles's narrow shoulders. "Somebody get his feet."

The boys hesitated for a moment.

Cruiser stepped in front of Kirkland. "What do we do if those mutants come back? What do we do then?"

Kirkland pushed Cruiser away and took Miles's feet. As they picked up Miles, he looked once more to the south.

# Two

Vinnie Pelligrino shook his head slowly. The red-haired, sixteen-year-old boy sat inside a hanging cage. It overlooked the bandit warriors' encampment on the beach of the hidden lagoon on Lost Island. The beach was covered with huts and sailing boats. Last night, the other boys had tried to rescue Vinnie and Joey Wolfe from Meat Hook's band, but they had failed.

Vinnie felt hatred and fear as he watched the weird assembly of bandits below him. Earlier that morning, they had killed Joey, the boy who had been captured along with Vinnie. The one named Cannibal had dragged the body away. Joey's head had been raised on a stake in the middle of the camp. Vinnie hadn't been able to bring himself to look at the bizarre spectacle.

The ragged-looking bandits moved back and forth on the beach. They were preparing for something, probably a counterattack on Vinnie's friends on Apocalypse Island. Kirkland and the others had done some damage, but Meat Hook and his men were as strong as ever. Kirkland had been lucky to last as long as he had against the superior forces of the bandits.

Meat Hook moved out from a tall grass hut to survey the progress of his army. The bandit leader had dark, shoulder-length hair. An American eagle had been tattooed on his chest. In his right hand, he clutched a sharp iron hook from which he took his name.

Meat Hook raised the hook over his head. A fat man in a studded leather vest and a rounded, polished steel helmet stepped up beside him. His name was Bullet Head, and he was Meat Hook's second in command.

Bullet Head picked up a large wooden mallet. He lifted the hammer and struck a huge gong in front of the hut, calling the others to order. They trudged through the camp and gathered in front of Meat Hook's headquarters.

"Brothers!" the bandit leader cried.

They cheered him. They were like a giant, dangerous animal in their single-minded thoughts of destruction.

Vinnie could not hear the orders Meat Hook gave, but the message was clear. The mutants were sworn to vengeance against Kirkland and the other castaways on Apocalypse Island.

Vinnie saw that Bullet Head was now holding

a large, army-green bag. It was marked with danger warnings because it was full of explosives.

Vinnie remembered the large eruption that had lit up the sky last night in the rescue attempt and attack. One of the boys in Kirkland's group had blown up the rocks at the entrance of the lagoon.

Vinnie watched the bandits move to the edge of the lagoon, with Meat Hook leading the way. Bullet Head carried the explosive charge over his shoulder. He was going to use the charge to reopen the secret channel that had been closed the night before.

Leaning back in the cage, Vinnie sighed, looking toward the blue sky. The previous night had been filled with fire and fury. Now a gentle breeze curled around him.

"Oh, Carrot-Top!"

Vinnie looked down and saw the hideous white face of the bandit named Cannibal. Cannibal stirred a huge, bubbling caldron. He leered up at Vinnie with hateful eyes.

"I need carrots for my stew," Cannibal said. "We're having you for lunch."

Vinnie gripped the bars of the cage. "Go ahead and kill me. Get it over with."

Cannibal waved his finger in a mocking gesture. "No, not yet. Meat Hook thinks you could become one of us."

"No way!" Vinnie cried. "I'd kill all of you if I had the chance. I'd cut your throats."

Cannibal grinned. "See? You're coming right along."

Vinnie turned toward the lagoon again. Bullet Head's boat was entering the hidden channel between the rocks. About thirty minutes later, an explosion resounded over the blue water. Smoke rose high in the air.

Another thirty minutes passed before the boat came back into the lagoon. Bullet Head signaled toward shore. The channel was clear.

Meat Hook waved his hand. The bandits hurried to their boats. A few minutes later, the mutant armada was launched.

Vinnie sighed, looking toward the sky. "They're dead," he muttered. "Dead meat."


Lieutenant Branch Colgan, a U.S. Coast Guard rescue pilot, moved quickly through the busy restaurant carrying an armful of charts and maps of the South Seas. It had taken him most of the morning to secure the maps from the aviation library in Honolulu. Colgan had then driven to this restaurant on the other side of town, so he would not be recognized.

Colgan eased into the booth and dropped the maps next to him. He ordered coffee, then glanced toward the entrance of the eatery. His co-conspirator had not yet arrived.

Colgan looked nervously at the charts. He had already been suspended from his duties as a pilot. Now he was risking his military career by staying on the trail of the missing plane. His superiors wanted to forget about the old C-47 because it had gone down in a restricted area. But Colgan could not forget until he had made an honest effort to find the plane and the missing passengers.

"Colgan."

A slender, aristocratic gentleman was standing in front of him. "Sir Charles, sit down," Colgan said.

Sir Charles Bookman, the famous British photojournalist, took the seat on the other side of the booth. Bookman's son, Miles, had been on the plane that went down in the storm. He was as determined as the young lieutenant to find the missing C-47.

Colgan leaned back in the booth. "There's something you don't know, Sir Charles. I haven't told you why the service wouldn't let me fly into the restricted area, the Omega quadrant."

"The Proteus Project," Sir Charles replied. "An effort to rehabilitate hardened criminals through a kind of serum. And there's reason to believe that some of those criminals might still be out there."

Colgan gaped in disbelief. "How did you—"

11

"I have my sources," Bookman replied. "I've been busy this morning."

"And you still want to go through with this?" Colgan asked.

Bookman nodded sadly. "I've failed my son in many ways, but I won't fail him again."

Colgan reached for the maps. He unfolded a chart and laid it flat on the table. Bookman leaned over to study the chart with him.

Colgan traced a large triangle in the sea of blue. "This is where I believe we should concentrate our effort."

Bookman nodded. "I agree."

"We'll need a plane."

"It can be done,"

Colgan leaned back. "I'll need a civilian pilot's license, preferably in another name."

"I have money," Bookman said. "Everything after that is easy. I'll spare no expense to find my son. I can pay you whatever you want, Lieutenant."

Colgan waved his hand. "No. No money for me. I just want to do my job. I want to find those kids, if—"

Bookman's eyes narrowed. "Go on, say it."

"If they're still alive," Colgan replied.

"Pray that they are, Lieutenant. Pray that they are."

# Three

As Kirkland bent to pick up Miles, a rumbling sound rolled over the water. All the boys looked to the south. The echo lasted for a few moments, then died away.

"What was that?" Cruiser asked.

"Thunder," Len replied. "A storm, maybe."

Kirkland looked at the clear sky. "Not a cloud. Come on—let's get him back to the lab."

Len and Kirkland carried Miles across the beach to the jungle path that led up to the compound. Len began to sweat as they trudged through the undergrowth.

Len glanced down at Miles's pitiful form. They had been classmates at Dover Academy in New Hampshire. Len wondered if they would ever get back there.

Cruiser stared back into the shadows of the dense growth. "I don't like this. Let's ditch him and get out of here!"

"Shut up!" Kirkland said. "Move it, Hayden. We don't have all day."

For a while, the jungle grew thicker around them. Len helped to navigate around the man-traps that they had set along the trail. The traps had sent several of Meat Hook's men to shallow graves in the jungle.

Augie hung back with Cruiser and D.J. Though Cruiser and D.J. were both bigger than Augie and Cruiser was older, Augie was the least afraid. He was even beginning to feel at home on the island.

The trail began to widen a little. Len and Kirkland carried Miles into a clearing that was full of orange trees. The fruit-laden grove had been planted by the men who had run the research project on Apocalypse Island. The oranges, like many things on the island, would not have grown there naturally.

Kirkland stopped. "Let's take a breather."

They lowered Miles to the ground. The arrow in his torso twitched with each rasping movement of his chest. Len's stomach was turning, and his legs had gone weak. He wrestled with the horrible reality that Miles might die.

Something rustled in the green growth above the orange trees. They all watched for signs of Dog Face, but the rustling quickly stopped and the morning shadows were still again.

Kirkland pointed up the trail. "Keep moving."

The trail slanted upward. They emerged from the trees at the base of a moss-and-vine-covered slope. A clear stream of water trickled down the incline and disappeared into the jungle below them.

Kirkland backed up the incline as Len followed, holding Miles's legs. They fought to maintain their balance as they ascended.

Kirkland turned to survey the small plateau between the jungle and the volcanic mountain behind the compound. The red-brown peak stood tall against the blue sky.

Cruiser and D.J. came over the edge of the plateau. They gawked at the two white buildings at the base of the mountain. They had not seen the compound before.

Cruiser read the writing on the sign. *Proteus Research and Development Center.* And painted over it—*Welcome to Apocalypse City.* "What does this mean?"

"Don't worry," Kirkland replied. "We'll get out of here soon enough. Come on, let's take him into the lab."

Len wasn't sure what Kirkland meant. Were Kirkland and the others planning to run off and leave him and Miles? They didn't seem to have much loyalty to anyone but themselves.

Cruiser, D.J., and Augie wandered over the

plateau, gaping in disbelief. The place was incredible. The mountain and the jungle had isolated the compound. The white buildings gleamed in the bright rays of the tropical sun.

"Unbelievable!" D.J. muttered.

Cruiser pointed toward the building. "Augie, is that where they made those mutants from the other island?"

Augie nodded. "Yes, the scientists did it."

"Where are the scientists now?" D.J. asked.

"I guess they left." Augie shrugged.

"This is too bugged out for me," D.J. said.

"We've got to help Miles," Augie said. "Then we can go."

They followed Len and Kirkland into the lab building. The older boys were already taking Miles down a flight of steps. Cruiser followed them into the lab basement, where they put Miles on a padded table.

Cruiser's head turned slowly. "What kind of place is this?"

Len turned quickly toward a blank concrete wall. *"Proteus!"*

When he spoke the word, the wall creaked. Cruiser jumped back as the concrete began to slide. The wall opened to reveal a hidden storage compartment. Shelves of supplies lined the secret chamber.

Cruiser was dumbfounded. "How'd you do that?"

"I discovered it by accident," Len replied. "My voice activates a mechanism that triggers the hidden wall."

Kirkland waved at the steps. "Cruiser, D.J., Augie—go to the edge of the compound and keep a look out for the mutants."

Cruiser hesitated. "Kirkland, I—"

"Go!"

Kirkland fixed his eyes on the aluminum arrow and reached toward Miles.

"What are you going to do?" Len asked quickly.

Kirkland scowled. "I'm going to get that arrow out of there." He tore away the bloody strips of Miles's T-shirt, then motioned toward the hidden compartment. "Get in there and find me something to clean this wound."

Len searched between the rows of shelves until he found a bottle of medicinal alcohol and a first-aid box that was filled with bandages. He took the supplies out to Kirkland.

A dark grimace had spread over the older boy's face. He was staring at the wound. Miles's whole body had turned deathly blue, but he was still alive.

"Give me that!"

Len handed Kirkland the bottle of alcohol. Kirkland poured the cool, clear liquid over the wound and the shaft of the arrow. The alcohol cut streaks in the dried blood that covered Miles's torso.

"Get me something to cut this arrow," Kirkland said.

Len looked around the lab until he found a pair of snipping pliers.

Kirkland doused the pliers with alcohol. "Man, I hope this works." He snipped off part of the arrow leaving about four inches of the shaft protruding from Miles's body. Then he pulled Miles toward the edge of the table.

"Help me here, prep."

"What are you going to do?" Len asked.

"I saw this in a movie once," Kirkland replied. "Here, hold him so he doesn't fall off."

Len held on to Miles as Kirkland poured more alcohol over the wound. Then he reached into his pocket for a plastic lighter. He touched the flame to the wet alcohol and a blue flame rose over the wound and the arrow. Kirkland then used the pliers to push the arrow all the way through Miles's body. When the tip of the shaft pierced the other side of his torso, Kirkland grabbed the arrow with the pliers and pulled the metal shaft clear of the wound.

Len quickly patted out the blue flames. "Kirkland—"

The older boy held up the tip of the arrow. "Look, prep. It has a barb on the end. If we'd taken it out any other way, it would have pulled his guts through with it."

Len grabbed the bottle and poured more alcohol into the wound. Blood oozed from the tiny circle. He dabbed at the opening with a piece of gauze from the first-aid box. The wound hardly seemed lethal now—the puncture mark looked small. But Miles's face was dark and hollow.

Kirkland threw the pliers and the arrow to the floor. "Put a bandage on him. There are some antibiotics around here somewhere." He started toward the steps.

"Where are you going?" Len asked.

Kirkland looked back over his shoulder. "We're leaving, Hayden. If you want to come along, get in the boat. We can sail into a shipping lane or something."

Len pointed toward Miles. "What about him?"

Kirkland shrugged. "Bring him when you've bandaged him. We won't leave him as long as he's alive."

"He's almost dead now," Len pleaded. "He won't survive if we take him along."

Kirkland scowled. "You don't have any choice, prep. If Bookman is going to survive, he has to take his chances like the rest of us. We're getting out of here before it's too late."

"It already is, Kirkland."

Augie stood above them on the steps, Commando at his side.

"What's wrong?" Len asked.

"Go see," Augie replied blankly. "I'll stay with Miles."

Len finished bandaging the wound and flew up the steps. The others were gathered at the edge of the plateau, staring at the water to the south.

Len rushed to them. His eyes grew wide when he saw the spectacle on the horizon.

"The mutants," Cruiser said. "There must be a hundred of them!"

"They're coming after us," Len said in a low voice.

Meat Hook's armada knifed through the water. The boats were still far away, but they would not take long to get to Apocalypse Island. The boys gaped at the dark specks on the calm blue surface of the ocean.

"We've got to do something, Kirkland! They'll be here soon." Cruiser's voice trembled.

Kirkland glanced nervously toward the beach. "Either we stay to face them, or we run."

"I vote to run," Cruiser replied.

D.J. nodded. "Me, too."

Len studied the encroaching fleet. "We'll never outrun them in the V-hull. They've got cats and lasers. Even if we caught the wind and the tide, they'd still get us."

A shiver ran through Kirkland's shoulders as the boats drew closer. If Meat Hook captured them, he would put them in cages like Vinnie and Joey.

"We gotta go!" Cruiser whined.

Len pointed at the lab building. "We can hide in the Proteus room. They'll never find us in there."

Sweat stung Kirkland's eyes. To him, the secret room was just another prison, dark and musty, closing him in. He would be just as trapped. "D.J., go get Augie," he said. "Tell him we're pulling out."

"Yes!" Cruiser yelled.

D.J. started to run, but Len stopped him.

"We have to take Miles," Len said. "We have to carry him down to the boat."

Kirkland shook his head. "He'll just slow us down. We've got to save our own hides."

Len could see the glint in Kirkland's eyes. He didn't care about Miles. He was going to save himself. But Len was not ready to give up.

Kirkland pushed D.J. toward the lab. "Get Augie. Tell him he can't bring the dog."

Len stepped in front of D.J. "No, I'll tell him."

"What's with you?" Kirkland asked.

"I'm staying," Len replied. "I'm not going to leave Miles. I'll hide with him in the Proteus room."

Kirkland sighed and shook his head.

"Just one thing," Len said. "If you make it back to civilization, tell someone we're out here."

Kirkland stared out at the water. "Sure. Anything you say. Now tell Augie we're pulling out."

He hurried through the lab and down the stairs. Augie and Commando were sitting next to the padded table where Miles lay.

Augie looked up. "Miles didn't wake up," he announced.

Len knelt next to the smaller boy. "Augie, Kirkland and the others are leaving. They say you can come along, but you can't bring Commando."

Augie lowered his head. "No. I'm staying with Miles. He needs us, Hayden. He'll die if we don't stay."

"The bandits are coming," Len offered in a gloomy tone. "You know what will happen if they find us."

Augie patted Commando's head. "I don't care. We're not afraid of anything."

"Are you sure?" Len asked.

Augie nodded. "I don't want to go home. I don't like it there. I want to stay here with Commando."

Len put his hand on Augie's shoulder. "Stay here with Miles while I go back and tell the others."

But when Len got outside, the others had already left. They were moving through the jungle, heading for the beach and the V-hull sailboat. They hadn't even waited for Augie.

Len walked to the edge of the plateau. Meat Hook's fleet was close enough that he could make out the puffy sails and toothpick masts. Soon the other boys emerged on the beach to launch the V-hull.

Len watched the bandits draw closer.

Frothy waves lapped over Kirkland's chest, almost knocking him into breaking surf. He clung tightly to the side of the V-hull sailboat. The three of them had to push the vessel past the waves to escape into the open sea.

A crashing breaker slapped the side of the boat, and Kirkland lost his grip. Suddenly he was under water, swirling with the current.

Kirkland pushed through the surface again and saw D.J. floating past him. He grabbed D.J. and pulled him back toward the boat. Kirkland caught hold of the side again.

"Cruiser!" he shouted.

"Back here," came the reply.

Kirkland saw Cruiser behind the V-hull. He lifted D.J. to the boat and gave him a push over the side. The younger boy flopped into the bottom.

"Raise the mast!" Kirkland cried.

D.J. didn't know what to do. Miles had been the sailor, but they had left him behind.

Kirkland and Cruiser turned the bow into the waves and began to push. Slowly the boat broke through the surf, gliding out into deeper water. The boys found themselves swimming behind the craft.

Suddenly D.J. stood up. "Hey, I think I found it."

D.J. pulled a loose line, and the mast shot up into the air. The luffing sail caught the offshore breeze and the vessel swung away from the island, heading due south toward Meat Hook's invading army.

"Lower the mast!" Kirkland cried.

D.J. let go of the line. The canvas fell flat into the bottom of the boat. As the vessel slowed, Kirkland pulled himself over the side, then reached back to haul Cruiser out of the water.

Now Meat Hook's forces were clearly visible. Kirkland had to get the V-hull into open water. Once there, they might cross the path of a ship or get spotted by a plane. It was better than waiting around to die.

Kirkland desperately tried to remember how Miles had sailed the boat. He pulled at the line that raised the mast. The sail billowed, and the offshore wind again pushed them toward the bandits.

"Wrong way!" Cruiser shouted.

Kirkland grabbed the tiller, trying to turn the boat around, but he couldn't change their course. He finally had to lower the sail.

The boat twirled helplessly until a strong current took hold and the bow turned due north. Suddenly, the V-hull was moving toward the other end of the island, away from the bandits.

"All right!" Kirkland yelled.

He let the V-hull flow with the tide. At least it was better than sailing straight for the bandits.

As Len watched Kirkland, Cruiser, and D.J. fumble with the boat, he silently urged them on. He wanted them to escape. If they got away from Meat Hook, they might get into a shipping lane and send help back to the island.

From his vantage point on the plateau, Len could see the mutant fleet approaching. He wondered if they would follow Kirkland and the others. If Meat Hook did not send any men ashore, Len and Miles and Augie would be safe for the moment.

He looked for the V-hull, but it was out of sight, having disappeared on the western side of the island, beyond the jutting crags of volcanic rock.

He gazed back at the armada. His chest burned as the mutants drew nearer. As they swung close to the southern tip of the beach, Len held his breath. But the boats didn't land.

Instead, the fleet swung away from the shore. Meat Hook pointed north. He had seen the V-hull trying to get away. The mutants followed their commander's lead.

Len watched in relief as the mutants disappear around the western shore, then ran quickly back to the lab to see Augie and Miles.

"How is he?" Len asked.

Augie shook his head. "I don't know. A couple of times I was scared that he died. But his chest is moving."

Len sighed. "Please, Miles. Don't die. Please."

Augie glanced toward the stairs. "What's happening up there?"

"The mutants are chasing Kirkland and the others."

Augie stared at the padded table. "That's what they get for leaving Miles. They should have stayed."

Len looked toward the Proteus room, which was still open. They should go ahead and hide. "Better safe than sorry"—wasn't that what his father always said?

"Augie, we've got to move Miles into the other room."

Augie stood up. "Okay."

The padded table didn't have wheels, so they had to slide the table into the hidden chamber. Food and water were stored in the compartment, enabling them to survive for quite some time.

Len motioned to Augie. "Come on."

Augie shook his head. "No. Good-bye, Len. We can't keep Commando here, and I won't leave him. I'll stay in the jungle."

Augie turned to run up the stairs, and Commando went after him. Len called, but he didn't want to chase the younger boy. He had to help Miles.

"Proteus."

The concrete wall closed, leaving them in darkness.


"They're on our tail!" Cruiser shouted. "Kirkland—"

"I see them!"

D.J. was speechless.

Kirkland glanced back over his shoulder. The line of boats was not far behind. Len had been right—they would never be able to outrun them.

"What are we going to do?" Cruiser whined.

Kirkland saw two of the bandit vessels breaking away from the pack. Laser boats knifed through the water, tacking to the side. Long, flashing blades reflected the sun as the lasers circled to build up speed. He looked back toward the island. They were near the north end.

If they could get to shore, they could try to hide in the mountains.

Kirkland desperately tried to steer, but the current kept taking them toward deeper water. Kirkland slammed his hand against the tiller in frustration.

Cruiser grabbed his forearm. "Here they come!"

The lasers had actually swung in front of the V-hull. The mutants were making their first pass with their swords.

Kirkland suddenly let out the sail, as the laser rushed down on them.

"Duck!" Kirkland cried.

As the boys ducked low, the blades slammed into the mast. The lasers shot by as the mast fell into the water. Kirkland looked up to see them circling again.

The current carried the V-hull away from the northwestern tip of the island. Kirkland let go of the tiller.

The lasers had almost completed their wide circle. The rest of the fleet was also drawing closer. Kirkland stared at his executioners, knowing that death was preferable to captivity.

# Four

Branch Colgan waited in the shaded alley, watching the brown door into which Sir Charles had disappeared. After breakfast, the Englishman had directed him to an old, seedy part of Honolulu. The streets were narrow and damp. Sir Charles had said that if you wanted to secure illegal items, you must go directly to the source.

The lieutenant flinched when the door creaked open. A large, dark man in a red shirt came out. He closed the door and started for the street. There was still no sign of Sir Charles.

Colgan sweated in the steamy air. He was nervous. He did not enjoy sneaking around. He preferred things straight and above board. But Colgan knew he had to go after those kids. They were somewhere in Omega quadrant. He could feel it with the same instincts that made him a good rescue pilot. All he wanted was a chance to find them.

The door creaked open again, and Sir Charles stepped out. Colgan shot across the alley.

"Did you get it?" he asked.

Sir Charles nodded toward the street. "In the car."

The walked out of the shadows and headed for the rented Chevy. Sir Charles got behind the wheel. Colgan climbed in on the passenger's side.

Sir Charles handed the lieutenant a large white envelope. "This is the best I could do."

Colgan opened the envelope and found a Hawaii driver's license and pilot's license under the name Cole Booker. He would need both of them when they rented the plane.

"Satisfactory?" Sir Charles asked.

Colgan nodded slowly. "I think they'll do."

"Good."

Sir Charles started the car and put it into gear. As they rolled away from the run-down neighborhood, the Englishman's face was grim.

"Something wrong?" Colgan asked.

Sir Charles exhaled. "Have you ever heard of Dr. Cyrus Albright?"

"No."

"He was the head of the Proteus Project," Sir Charles replied. "He developed the serum used in the experiments."

"What's that got to do with us?" Colgan asked.

Sir Charles stared straight ahead into traffic as

he spoke. "The man who got those documents for me had some disturbing news. I had asked him to check on Albright for me." He paused. "Three weeks ago, the good doctor checked himself out of a sanitarium in California. He was a voluntary committal, so the doctors there couldn't stop him from leaving."

"I still don't see—"

Sir Charles held up his hand. "Let me finish. A week after he left the hospital, a ship disappeared from the navy yard in San Diego."

Colgan's brow fretted. "Disappeared?"

"One morning it was there, the next it was gone without a trace. It just seemed to vanish into thin air. The navy yard was maximum security," the Englishman went on. "But the thief still got the boat out of the yard. The boat happens to have been the mother ship of the Proteus Project. It had been there in mothballs for years."

"And you think Albright stole it?"

"I do," Sir Charles replied. "He's a man of extraordinary intelligence. He worked for a while on the neutron bomb. He's a genius of sorts, though he has had bouts with mental illness."

Colgan shook his head. "So he stole this boat. Do you think he's going back to the island where those experiments took place?"

"Where else would he be going?" Sir Charles replied.

Colgan was quiet for a moment. On the one hand, the doctor might help the boys if he found them stranded in Omega quadrant. On the other, a deranged genius was now heading straight into the territory they were going to search.

"We better hurry," Colgan said.

"Where can we get a plane?" Sir Charles asked.

"On the other side of the island," Colgan replied. "It's going to cost plenty if we don't want any questions asked."

"Let me worry about that," Sir Charles said. "You just find my son."

The lasers sped straight toward the V-hull from both sides. Kirkland pushed Cruiser and D.J. into the bottom of the boat. Then he grabbed the sail that floated in the water and pulled it toward him until he had recovered the boat's fallen mast.

D.J. raised his head to look at the lasers. "They're coming!" he cried hysterically. Kirkland swung the mast around in front of him. The V-hull was now floating in a strong current that pushed them west. The lasers had the wind at their backs, so they were only a few seconds away from attacking.

Kirkland held tight to the mast. He had the angle on the lasers. He could see their dirty monkey-like faces behind the weapons. Their yellow eyes taunted him. The silver blades flashed in their hands.

"Come on," Kirkland said. "Come and get what you deserve."

At least he could go down fighting. He focused his dark eyes on the laser that rushed in from the right. When the craft was on top of them, Kirkland raised the mast and used it like a jousting knight uses a lance.

The tip of the mast caught the bandit in the middle of his chest and knocked him into the water. The empty boat rushed by the V-hull.

Then the other laser rushed in from the left side. Kirkland tried to come over with the mast, but the fallen bandit had swum to the edge of the V-hull, and his hand now grabbed the side of the boat. His blade also came over the rail.

D.J. grabbed the hand with the sword and sank his teeth into the rough fingers. The bandit screeched, letting go of the sword. The long-bladed weapon fell into the bottom of the V-hull.

Kirkland picked up the saber. The bandit's hands returned to the side of the boat. Kirkland sank the tip of the blade into the soft part of the bandit's throat. The man made a gurgling sound and drowned in a slick of his own blood.

"You got him!" D.J. cried.

Kirkland looked up. The other bandits were coming closer, riding the swift current to the west.

"Why don't they just get it over with!" D.J. cried.

Kirkland grimaced. "The cat always plays with the mouse before it kills it. Meat Hook is messing with our heads again. He doesn't want to kill us right now. He wants to lock us up in a cage."

A catamaran cut out of the pack to join the remaining laser. The two craft met for a few moments. Something changed hands, and the boats circled back toward the castaways.

The V-hull was still riding the flow of the tide. Kirkland could see the northwestern tip of the island. He had been there with Len and Miles before, when the pair of mutants had attacked them.

He looked back at the fleet. Meat Hook and his men were less than a hundred yards away, forming a semicircle around them. They could never make it to shore in time to hide.

Kirkland had the saber in hand, ready to duel.

The laser and the catamaran made their attacking run. Kirkland could see the glinting of oil on the barrel of a pistol. The bandits had guns now.

Kirkland still held the saber in front of him. He was not going to cower like a frightened rat.

He would fight to the death rather than face one of those bamboo cages.

"Come on, fight like men!"

Kirkland glared at the catamaran. An ugly man with a scarred face lifted the barrel of the pistol. A puff of smoke escaped from the barrel, and Kirkland heard the report of the weapon. The lead slug sped through the water in front of the V-hull. The first volley had fallen short.

A second shot erupted from the laser, which was knifing in from the other side. The slug smashed against the side of the boat. The vessels were closing in on them.

Kirkland watched as the pistol was lifted again. The mutant was aiming at him. It would be all over when he pulled the trigger.

But the shot never came. Something whistled over the V-hull. Suddenly, the catamaran exploded in a thousand pieces. A few seconds later, the laser went up in a ball of flames.

Cruiser lifted his head. "What happened?"

A series of eruptions all around the V-hull left the air filled with dense smoke. Kirkland and the others floated into the cloak of the smoky vapor. Dark mists swirled around them. The explosions continued for a few more seconds. The cloud had become so thick that the boys were hidden from the view of the bandit fleet.

"What is it?" D.J. whined.

"Shut up."

Kirkland listened intently. The sound of a whirring engine echoed through the smoke. Another ship had arrived in the shroud.

The bow of the larger vessel towered over their small boat. The word *Proteus* loomed out at them from the mist. Something emerged from the smoke, and suddenly the boys were tangled in a thick net. It seemed to swallow them up, closing from the bottom. They were lifted out of the boat seconds before the V-hull exploded in the water.

Kirkland tried to cut the netting, but he dropped the saber in the process. The boys hung over the side of the larger vessel in a heap. There was nothing they could do as the *Proteus* turned sharply and sped toward shore.

# Five

Meat Hook's men searched through the smoke for a long time before they found the wreckage of the V-hull. They had heard the sound of running engines in the cloud, but they had not seen the boat itself. By the time the vapor lifted, there was no sign of the vessel.

Bullet Head stared dumbly at the floating debris. "They're dead."

He raised his hands in triumph. The other bandits cheered like chattering monkeys. Their enemy had been vanquished.

Meat Hook raised a hand to stop their celebration. His red-streaked eyes were turned to the horizon. Something was not right. The explosions had not been the work of his men.

"Who did this?" Meat Hook cried.

Bullet Head frowned.

"He's back," Meat Hook said blankly. "He has returned."

Bullet Head's fat face showed recognition. "No!"

"Who else?" Meat Hook said. "He has come back to face his children."

"We can finally kill him!" Bullet Head cried.

They cheered loudly. Suddenly the boys were forgotten. The bandits had another target in mind.

Meat Hook pointed his iron claw toward the south. "Home—we must prepare to receive our father. He has returned."

The fleet began to tack, making for Lost Island. As they sailed the western shore of the land mass that had once been their home, none of them heard the shouting from the beach of Apocalypse Island.

But the bandits were too far offshore to see or hear their brother, Dog Face. They left him on the island, stranded with Len and Miles.

Cruiser screamed when the boat began to rise out of the water. The *Proteus* was a hydrofoil vessel, capable of running at great velocity on three outrigger-skis. In five minutes, the craft had run beyond the horizion line, and the visibility of the bandits.

The boys hung in the net, bouncing around like captive fish. Cruiser continued to cry, and D.J. whimpered until Kirkland told them both to be quiet.

The *Proteus* slowed and dropped into the water again. The engines idled as the sea lapped against the hull. On top of the vessel, a radar dish turned in a circle, marking the position of the bandit fleet. The *Proteus* would not return to the island until Meat Hook was out of range.

Cruiser tried to turn his face toward the vessel. "Let us out of this net. Please!"

Kirkland squirmed against the mesh. "Let us go! We're lost. Our plane crashed."

D.J. whimpered, but his words were incoherent.

But the low idling of the engines was the only reply. After a few minutes, something dropped into the net from above. A round metal canister began to billow out a noxious smoke. In a few seconds, all the boys lost consciousness. They hung limply in the net as the boat began to move toward the island once again.

In the darkness of the secret chamber, Len Hayden sat against the concrete wall, listening to Miles's shallow breathing. Len knew there was nothing more he could do for his friend. He could only wait and wonder when they could leave the hidden room. He didn't like sitting in the black void, but he figured that at least he was safe.

When they had discovered the Proteus room, it was untouched, as if the scientists had left it intact on purpose. The mutants had never disturbed it, which suggested that they didn't know about it. Even if Meat Hook came ashore and searched the lab now, there was a good chance that they would not be able to open the door. Sitting in the dark was better than dying or being hung in a bamboo cage.

Len closed his eyes. He tried to think about home, but fatigue overtook him. He slept for a long time, then woke to Miles's violent coughing.

Miles thrashed about on the padded table and cried out deliriously. Len jumped up, fumbling in the darkness.

"Hang on, Bookman. You're going to be okay."

"Hurts," Miles said softly. "Hurts bad."

Reaching into the first-aid box, Len found some pain-killers and managed to get Miles to swallow two of the pills. Miles thrashed for a while before he fell back into a fitful sleep.

Len leaned back against the wall. Suddenly, something clumped behind him. He froze. He heard movements in the outer lab area. The mutants had come ashore.

Another loud thump made the walls tremble, and the whine of an engine stirred to life deep in the bowels of the lab. A dim red light came on over Len's head. Meat Hook had turned on the electricity!

Len put his ear to the wall. Someone was moving across the floor. Even through the concrete, Len heard the word spoken.

"Proteus!"

The concrete wall began to slide open. Len stepped back to stand in front of Miles. He groped for a weapon to fend off the bandits and found a large glass bottle.

But there were no bandits standing in the lab basement. An older gentleman in a white linen suit turned to look at Len. He did not seem surprised to see the boy. His gray eyes were narrow and piercing.

He pointed a crooked finger at Len. "Put that down immediately," he said in a deep voice seasoned by an Eastern European accent.

Len waved the bottle. "Stay away from me!"

"Please," the man replied in a friendly tone. "The bottle contains a highly corrosive acid that will eat through your skin."

Len lowered the bottle. He studied the man's pointed face, which was covered by round, wire-rimmed spectacles. He was almost bald, and his frame was pudgy. Sweat-stains soaked the linen of his coat. He kept his gray eyes focused on Len.

"Put the bottle on the shelf, young man. You wouldn't want to drop it."

Len reached back and did as the man instructed. Then he turned to look again at the

**41**

older gentleman. Somehow the intruder did not seem frightening.

The man waved a hand at Len. "Now, move out into the lab so I can get a look at you."

Len shook his head. "My friend is hurt. I can't leave him."

The man frowned. "Hurt? Perhaps I can help him." He took a step toward the padded table.

Len stuck out his hand, stopping him. "Who are you? How did you get here?"

The man clicked his heels like royalty. "Ah yes, introductions are in order. My name is Dr. Cyrus Albright. Now, let's have a look at your friend."

# Six

The rental car rolled slowly down the dark, narrow road that led into the mountains. Branch Colgan was behind the wheel. Sir Charles Bookman sat in the passenger seat, gazing out at the dense green tropical growth on either side of the car. High, plant-covered slopes rose toward the night sky, blocking the view of the moon and the stars.

The car rolled up a steep incline. As it emerged over the crest of a hill, the headlights flashed on two dark structures in the distance. Colgan stopped the car. He turned off the lights and the engine.

"Is this it?" Sir Charles asked.

Colgan peered toward the shapes in the darkness. "I'm not sure. But if it is, he knows we're here. These natives can be funny about strangers. If we—"

Something clicked on the right side of the car.

Sir Charles turned toward the noise. Suddenly cold metal pressed against his skin. The barrel of a rifle rested on his neck.

A calm voice rose in the night. "You're a long way from home, gentlemen."

Colgan looked past the Englishman. "Billy? Billy Lopaca?"

"Who wants to know?"

Colgan figured he had better not give his real name, not with the bogus licenses in his pocket. "I'm a friend of Jim Antley. I was here once before. We took your plane up."

"Why you come now?" Lopaca asked.

"We want to talk to you," Colgan replied. "Can we come up?"

After a silent moment, Lopaca lifted the gun barrel from Sir Charles's neck. "Okay," he replied. "Come to the house. Leave the car here."

He started across the ridge toward a shack. Colgan and Sir Charles climbed out of the car.

"Not what I would call a pleasant host," the Englishman said.

"He does have a plane," Colgan replied.

They strode across the ridge. Billy Lopaca was sitting on the porch of the shack with the gun resting on his lap. He waited for Colgan to start talking.

"We want to hire your plane," the lieutenant said.

Lopaca frowned, his face barely visible in the

dim light that spilled from the windows of the shack. "Why?"

Colgan shrugged. "For island hopping."

"How long?"

"Two weeks, maybe more."

Lopaca laughed. "Cost you plenty."

"Name your price," Sir Charles said.

Lopaca gave a mocking chortle. "Ten thousand a week."

Sir Charles pointed toward the car. "I have thirty thousand dollars in a suitcase. We'll take the plane for three weeks."

Lopaca stopped laughing. "You serious?"

Sir Charles sighed impatiently and started to turn away. "Come on, Lieutenant. Let's find someone who wants to make a few dollars. I'm sure there's someone on this island with a plane to rent."

Colgan started to turn away.

"Wait," Lopaca said. "Don't go. I have a plane."

Colgan smiled. Sir Charles had executed a perfect bluff. Lopaca took the rifle off his lap and leaned it against the wall.

"I didn't know you were serious," Lopaca said.

Sir Charles nodded. "We're serious, but we don't have a lot of time to dilly-dally. We're offering a fair price."

"Too fair," Lopaca replied. "You got a license?"

Colgan reached into his pocket. "Right here. Take a look."

Lopaca perused the license in the dim light. "Your name was different the last time you were here. You're doing something illegal."

"We're searching for my son," Sir Charles replied. "He was lost in a plane wreck."

"Sure you are," Lopaca replied, handing the license back to Colgan.

Sir Charles gestured toward the car. "Let's go. We've wasted enough time with this—"

Lopaca stood up. "No! You can have the plane. Twenty-five hundred a week. Take it or leave it."

Sir Charles nodded. "We'll take it for four weeks."

"Done!" Lopaca replied, extending his hand.

Sir Charles shook to seal the deal.

"When can we have the plane?" Colgan asked.

Lopaca laughed again. "Sunrise. It'd be too dangerous to take off before then. That good enough for you, English?"

"Yes," Sir Charles replied. "That will be fine."

Dr. Cyrus Albright took another step toward Miles. Len stayed beside the padded table, protecting the wounded boy. He was not ready to trust the doctor to treat his friend.

"Stay away from him!" Len shouted.

Albright sighed. "Young man, what is your name?"

"Hayden. Len Hayden. And this is Miles Bookman. We were lost in a plane crash."

"I see," the doctor replied. "And how was your friend hurt?"

Len hesitated. "He was shot with an arrow. Kirkland got it out, but he's still weak."

"Kirkland?" the doctor asked. "Was he one of three young men in the sailboat?"

Len gaped at the older man. "Yes. How did you know about them?"

Albright made a *tsk*ing noise and waved his finger. "I know a great many things, Mr. Hayden. For one thing, I know that your friend must be in danger of losing his life."

Albright did not sound threatening to Len. He was more like a friendly instructor.

"Am I correct, Mr. Hayden? Is your friend in grave danger?"

"Well, yes," Len replied. "He's—"

Albright gestured to himself. "I'm a doctor, my young friend. A qualified surgeon and physician. I have degrees from three major universities in Europe and America. I might be able to help Miles, but you have to let me examine him."

Len moved slowly away from the padded table. Albright leaned over and studied the wound for a long time.

**47**

Then he shook his head, and leveled his gray eyes at Len. "There may be some internal bleeding. I may have to operate on Mr. Bookman to stop it."

"Operate? Open him up?"

"Yes, if you want him to live."

The doctor walked across the lab. He seemed to know his way around the place. Albright stopped dead when he saw the stacks of computer readouts on the lab table. He fingered the edges of the paper.

"Who was reading this log?" Albright asked.

"Miles," Len replied.

Albright smiled, gazing back at the wounded boy. "He must be a very bright boy to decipher these records."

Len's eyes widened with recognition. "Wait a minute! It was you! You're the one who ran the experiments on this island! You—"

Albright slumped over. Suddenly his face grew pale and his whole body began to shake. Reaching out, he steadied himself against the lab table. From the inside pocket of his linen coat, he took out a pill box and popped two tablets into his mouth.

"Are you all right?" Len asked.

The doctor nodded weakly. Sweat poured down his face, and he sat down for a moment on a lab stool. His lips moved as he muttered incoherently to himself.

**48**

"Dr. Albright?"

No response.

"Doctor?"

Dr. Albright seemed to come to life again. "Yes, Mr. Hayden. In answer to your question, I was one of the men responsible for the atrocities that took place on this cursed island. I am guilty as charged."

"Where did you come from? Have you been on the island all this time?"

Albright waved his trembling hand. "That's not important, young man. We must help your friend now. We must save his life, or my coming here will have been in vain."

"Do you have a boat?" Len asked. "Or a plane? Can you take us away from this place?"

Albright did not reply. He muttered to himself in a grim inner dialogue.

"You have to help us," Len went on. "There's a gang of bandits on the island to the south. Meat Hook is the leader."

"That's what he calls himself now?"

"You know him?"

Albright sighed. "When I knew him, he went by the name of Harry Stern. Our project reclaimed him from the California penitentiary system. Stern murdered seventeen people, including a family of four. He was the perfect subject for our experiments."

"Bullet Head! Do you know him? He's fat and ugly."

Albright waved his hand. "I can't remember his name, but his face has haunted my dreams a thousand times."

"Why did you leave them out here? Why didn't you take them back to prison?"

The doctor shook his head. "It was not my decision to leave them here. Certain men in the government have been unable to admit their mistakes. But I have returned to right my wrongs. Can you understand that, Len Hayden? Can you believe that I want to overturn the rock and destroy what's beneath it?"

Len grabbed the doctor's arm. "You've got to help us! You've got to take us back to civilization! Meat Hook will kill us all if he gets the chance. I bet he's already killed Kirkland and the others."

Albright stood up slowly and tried his legs, which were strong again. He moved through the lab, opening drawers and cabinets. He seemed to be searching for something.

"Patience, my young friend. Rome was not built in a single revolution of the sundial. You must give me time."

"We don't have time," Len replied. "Meat Hook will be coming for us. He hates us. He'll be storming the beach any minute."

"No, not right away," Albright said with confidence.

"How can you be sure?" Len asked.

Albright did not tell Len that he had monitored the movement of the bandit fleet with his radar as they returned to Lost Island. They were safe for a while.

Miles began to cough violently. Len turned toward the padded table, where Miles thrashed in the throes of some dark nightmare. He screamed with the pain that wracked his body. Len had to restrain him to keep him from falling off the table.

"All right, doctor. Help him if you can!"

Albright stood next to the padded table. His hand went into his pocket again, and he took another tablet from the pill box.

"Hold his mouth open," he told Len. "Hurry."

Len obeyed, and Albright dropped the pill into Len's mouth. Len started to give Miles some water.

"No!" Albright said. "He has a stomach wound. Giving him water might make him worse. Let him relax. He'll swallow the pill."

After a few minutes, Miles was calm again. But his breathing was still shallow.

"He's getting worse," Len said sadly.

Albright studied the puncture wound, which oozed a dark liquid. "We have to search for my instruments. We must sterilize them before I operate on him."

"You aren't operating on anyone!"

Len and Albright turned toward the stairs. Neil Kirkland stood at the bottom of the steps, with Cruiser and D.J. behind him.

Len gasped. "Kirkland—"

"Shut up. This old guy isn't going to touch Bookman."

Kirkland took a threatening step toward the table. He held a big club in his hand. Cruiser and D.J. also held blunt weapons. They were glaring at Dr. Cyrus Albright as if they wanted to bash in his skull.

Vinnie Pelligrino squinted between the bamboo bars of his cage. Nightfall made it hard for him to see the whirling shadows in the camp. As soon as the fleet had returned to the hidden beach, Meat Hook had put the mutants to work on some awful undertaking. They had not stopped since, moving quickly under the torchlight.

Cannibal stirred his caldron. The white-faced ghoul rarely left the flames of the fire. Vinnie had never seen him sleep.

"Oh, it is a fine day. The return of our glorious creator, our one father."

Vinnie scowled at the night sky. "What are you talking about?"

"Ah, that does smell divine! Would you like to taste it for me, Carrot-Top?"

Vinnie stared out at the camp again. He was

glad that the mutants had returned to Lost Island without any prisoners. That meant Kirkland might still be alive. He could bring help and get Vinnie out of the cage.

Cannibal banged a steel triangle, the dinner bell for the army. A ringing pealed through the camp. The men stopped working and filed by the caldron, taking the plates from Cannibal's skinny hand.

As they ate, Vinnie studied their hideous nightmarish faces. They had painted themselves with pagan symbols that could only have been imagined by a savage mind. Vinnie actually liked some of the designs.

Meat Hook and Bullet Head stared up at the cage. Bullet Head whispered something to his leader, but Meat Hook shook his head. They were probably deciding Vinnie's sorry fate.

Meat Hook pointed his iron weapon at him. "I have not forgotten you! You will be the offering to our father."

"Psycho!" Vinnie shouted.

Bullet Head frowned. "You have no manners."

Vinnie glared through the bars, his face pressed against the cage. "You can't get away with this. You'll pay."

"Silence!" Meat Hook cried.

"Give him to me," Bullet Head rejoined. "I'll break him."

"Soon," Meat Hook replied. "Soon."

The bandit leader stomped off toward his tent. Bullet Head leered at Vinnie, then turned to follow his master. They disappeared inside Meat Hook's grass hut.

"Oh, you'll be a fine offering," Cannibal said with a lilting tone. "A lamb to slaughter."

"Great," Vinnie said blankly. "Just great."

He leaned back against the bars of the cage. After a while, he heard the bandits working. He peered out into the spotty patches of torchlight.

They seemed to be making some kind of platform. Vinnie wondered if it was meant to support a huge weapon—or perhaps it was meant to serve as the altar for a sacrifice.


Kirkland tapped the club in the palm of his hand. "You aren't operating on Bookman, old man. You're going to answer some questions."

Dr. Albright sighed disgustedly. "I should have let them capture you."

"We woke up on the beach," Kirkland said. "And I think you had something to do with it."

"He's a doctor," Len said. "He can help Miles. Let him operate, Kirkland."

Ignoring Len, the dark-haired boy pointed the club at Albright. "Where's your gang?"

"I am alone," Albright replied.

Kirkland smashed a lab stool with the club, shattering it into small pieces. "You're lying! Nobody could have rescued us like that alone. You've got a crew stashed with your ship."

"Ship?" Len asked. "You have a ship?"

"He saved us from Meat Hook," Kirkland said. "Laid down smoke on the water, and came in to get us. He threw a net over us and gassed us to sleep. Next thing we know, we're barfing on the beach."

"I am sorry," Albright said wryly. "That particular gas always causes nausea as a side effect."

Kirkland pointed the club at the doctor. "You admit that you gassed us?"

Albright sighed. "I could not leave you for those savages. And I did not have time to reason with you. How are you feeling now?"

"Shut up," Kirkland replied. "Where'd you come from? How'd you just appear out of nowhere?"

Albright's eyes narrowed. "Mr. Kirkland, this young man may die if I don't operate immediately. I suggest that you do not impede my duties."

Kirkland put the club on the doctor's shoulder. "Answer me first, old man! How'd you pull off that smoke-bomb number?"

The doctor removed the club. "I was hiding in a cove on the western side of the island, inside the high cliffs. I saw everything on my instruments. I launched the smoke bombs, then used my radar to find you in the cloud. By the time the smoke cleared, the *Proteus* was beyond the horizon line."

"Why'd you destroy our boat?" Cruiser demanded.

"So the pirates would think you had perished," Albright replied. "I doubt if it worked."

Kirkland had a blank expression on his dumb face. "You did all this by yourself? Impossible."

"The *Proteus* is a remarkable ship," Albright said. "Now, if you'll excuse me, I have a patient to attend."

Albright moved toward the padded table, but Kirkland put the butt of the club in the doctor's chest and pushed him backward.

"I would advise you not to touch me again, Mr. Kirkland. It might force me to hurt you."

Kirkland laughed. "I'm trembling. You're gonna hurt me? You're losing it, old man! I'm in charge here."

"Let him help Miles," Len pleaded.

"Why'd you come back here?" Kirkland asked.

Albright slipped his hand into his coat pocket. "I was part of what took place here," he replied. "I have returned to set things straight."

"Where's the boat?" Kirkland demanded. "Where'd you stash it?"

"I cannot tell you that."

Kirkland waved the club under his chin.

"You're taking us out of here. Now where's the boat?"

"You could never find it," Albright replied. "Even if I gave you directions, you would not have the mental capacity to retain the complicated procedure."

"You calling me stupid?" Kirkland asked.

Albright seemed to be losing his patience. "This is ridiculous. I must operate on this young man before he dies." He took another step toward the table.

Kirkland held the club across Albright's chest. "Take us to the ship now," Kirkland demanded. "We're getting off this island."

Albright took several steps backward, his hand still in his coat pocket. "No regard for the life of your friend. Are you really that selfish?"

"Bookman's got one foot in the dumper already," Kirkland replied. "We're alive. You're smart enough to figure out the rest, old man. If you don't tell me where the boat is, I'll beat it out of you."

"No," Albright replied.

Kirkland lunged for the doctor. Albright lifted a round, circular object, and a projectile sprung from the older man's hand. Two metal prongs lodged in Kirkland's broad chest.

Kirkland cried out and twitched violently. His eyes fell back in his head as he tumbled to the floor.

"You killed him!" Cruiser shouted.

"No," Albright replied, "I gave him a stunning jolt of electricity. He'll be awake in an hour or so."

"A stun-gun!" Len cried with hope.

The doctor drew back his hand, and the metal prongs flew out of Kirkland's skin. Len could see in Albright's hand the thin wires that had conducted the electricity from the transformer.

The doctor pointed to Kirkland. "Get him out of here immediately. I don't want him to wake up in here while I'm operating."

Cruiser and D.J. grabbed Kirkland's limp body and dragged him up the stairs.

Len smiled at Albright. "You handled them."

"We must protect ourselves, Mr. Hayden. Do not move. This will take only a moment."

Albright walked to the base of the stairs and looked up at the ceiling. He cleared his throat, waved his hand, and said a single word: "Fortress!"

The lab basement began to vibrate. Two vents opened on the ceiling over the stairwell. Broad, flat gates of aluminum dropped quickly to the floor, sealing off the stairs.

"We're trapped!" Len said.

"No," Albright replied, "we are safe. The others will leave us in peace while we help your friend. Come, we must prepare."

Albright whirled around the lab with surprising agility. He helped Len pull the padded table under some bright lights that were attached to the lab's wall. Dark liquid still oozed from Miles's side.

"I left some surgical instruments here," Albright said as he pulled open a drawer.

They soaked the instruments in alcohol. Albright muttered to himself from time to time. His eyes were always glassy, and his face grew paler with each moment.

He picked up a clean scalpel. "You may want to look away, Mr. Hayden. There will be a lot of blood."

Len tried to watch, but his stomach turned over and he had to sit down. Albright seemed to labor forever on the operation. He finally put the last stitch in the incision.

Len looked over the doctor's shoulder. "How is he?"

Albright sighed and sat down himself. "There was no serious damage to his organs. He lost some blood. He . . ."

The old man's voice trailed off, and he began to sweat. He fumbled with the pill box and swallowed another tablet.

"Are you all right, Doctor?"

Albright stared blankly at the floor. His lips moved, but he did not seem to be saying anything. Finally, his eyes lifted to Len.

"Doctor? Are you all right?"

He nodded. "Yes. Your friend—"

"How is Miles?"

"Morning," Albright replied. "We should know something by morning."

Len leaned back against the wall. He closed his eyes, and in a few minutes he was asleep. He did not see the doctor reach into the inside pocket of his linen coat.

Albright took out a hypodermic needle. He filled it from a small bottle then put the bottle back in his coat. Raising the needle, he made sure the air was gone before he slipped the point into Miles's arm.

"Now, Mr. Bookman, let's see if you respond to my serum."

He pushed down the plunger, injecting the liquid into Miles's pale blue body.

# Seven

In the first light of morning, Sir Charles Book-man studied the airplane in front of him. "Colgan, you can't be serious. This C-47 is probably in worse shape than the one that crashed."

Branch Colgan was pulling on his flight jacket. "Don't let the appearance fool you. Billy has a nephew who works for Lockheed. Every bolt on this plane is tight. It has special modifications that advance the fuel capacity. I can make it all the way to Majoru without refueling."

Sir Charles shook his head. The plane seemed to be held together with spit and matchsticks.

"Colgan, when we—"

"There is no " 'we,' " Colgan replied. "You're not coming with me."

Sir Charles frowned. "But—"

"Someone has to stay back here," Colgan went on. "If you aren't here to back me up, your boy will be lost for sure. If I don't come back, you have to tell someone. Nobody else knows I'm doing this."

"What about Lopaca?"

Colgan glanced back toward the shack. "Billy has his money. He probably doesn't care if he ever sees me again."

Sir Charles saw the logic in Colgan's appeal. Somebody had to remain behind. He would have to trust the lieutenant to find his son.

"You need money for fuel," the Englishman said.

He handed Colgan an envelope that contained fifty one-hundred-dollar bills.

"How do you plan to proceed?"

"Work my way west," Colgan replied. "I'll island hop. There are places to refuel, so I should be able to give it a thorough search. I'll keep in touch."

Sir Charles nodded. He turned to the south, gazing across the plateau. A narrow strip of road stretched toward the edge of a steep cliff.

Colgan got inside the cockpit of the C-47, and the plane's engines sputtered to life.

He moved down the runway. The C-47 picked up speed as it headed for the edge of the plateau. Sir Charles heard the engines coughing when the plane went off the cliff. It fell for a moment, gliding toward the green valley below.

"Come on, Lieutenant. You can do it."

The plane leveled off over the trees, heading

straight for the base of the mountains in the distance. Colgan turned the nose upward, but Sir Charles wondered if he would make it over the high peaks.

"Faster!"

Suddenly the C-47 climbed at a steep angle. The tail cleared the peaks by several feet. Colgan flew the plane due west, out over the open blue ocean.

"Good show," Sir Charles muttered to himself.

He silently prayed that the young pilot would have a successful mission.

Len was back in the belly of the C-47. Miles sat next to him, holding his bookbag against his chest. Below the plane, Len could see the storm-tossed waters of the Pacific. Suddenly the plane was down in the water.

Len had to fight his way out of the sinking plane. His lungs ached until he burst through the surface of the water. As he floated on the waves, he heard someone calling to him.

The voice seemed to belong to Miles. "Hayden!"

Ahead of him on the waves, Miles struggled for his life. The sea swelled, taking him upward on the frothy crest. Len reached out, but he could not stop the sea from swallowing up his friend.

"Hayden!"

Len opened his eyes. It had been a dream, a bizarre replay of the plane crash that had left him stranded. He sat up.

"Hayden!"

Len looked for the doctor, but he didn't see Albright.

"Hayden, look at me."

His ears were playing tricks on him. Miles wasn't calling out to him. It was only his imagination, an echo of the dream.

"Hayden!"

Len eased toward the padded table. Miles's skin now had a rosy pink pallor. The circles under his eyes were gone. Len stopped dead when he saw Miles staring up at him.

"You're alive!"

"Hayden," Miles said, "get over here!"

Len leaned over. Maybe it was still part of the dream.

He stared down at the clear eyes. Miles was alert. He actually seemed like himself again.

"It's hot in here," Miles complained. "Open a window."

"How do you feel?" Len asked.

Miles's eyes narrowed. "My side hurts. What happened? I don't remember anything."

Len supplied the details.

Miles tried to sit up, but the pain was too great.

"Take it easy," Len said. "You were wounded pretty bad."

Sweat poured off Miles's face. His fever had broken, and the scar on his torso had stopped oozing.

"You were almost dead," Len said. "It's a miracle!"

"Not quite, Mr. Hayden. But close."

Dr. Albright stepped out of the Proteus chamber. He walked toward Miles, who squinted at the older man. Albright examined Miles, then nodded his head.

"Is he all right?" Len asked.

"He has recovered nicely," the doctor replied. "But we must be careful. He has to regain his strength."

"Len said I was almost a goner," Miles rejoined. "Thanks for saving me, Dr. Albright."

Albright insisted that the wound was not as bad as he had figured, but inside he rejoiced that his serum had performed the intended miracle.

"Your young constitution is strong," Albright said. "You're on your way to a full recovery."

"Amazing," Len said. "You did it!"

"Can you sit up, Mr. Bookman?"

"I'll try," Miles replied. But he soon grew dizzy and weak.

Dr. Albright helped him recline. "It's quite all right, Mr. Bookman. Soon you will be up and around. You have my guarantee."

Miles frowned at the man. "Do I know you? I mean, before?"

Albright smiled. "You should. According to Len, you were reading my records before I arrived."

"The Proteus Project!" Miles said. "You were the head of the experiments!"

Albright lowered his eyes. "And I have come back to undo my atrocities. If you and Mr. Hayden assist me, I will see to it that you are taken back to civilization, safe and sound."

Miles suddenly had a lot of questions. "What did you—"

Albright waved his hand impatiently. "I will tell you everything in due time, Mr. Bookman. Here, I'll give you something to lessen the pain you are feeling."

Miles shook his head. "No drugs. But I could sure use some water."

Len got a jug of fresh water from the storage area in the Proteus chamber. Albright cautioned Miles against drinking too much. Miles lowered his head after a couple of swallows.

"Thanks," he said softly. "Thanks for everything."

His eyes closed. In a few minutes, Miles was snoring.

Albright smiled at Len. "I would like some breakfast. Are you hungry?"

Len nodded, pointing to the shelves. "There

are freeze-dried packages. We could heat something over a burner."

"I was thinking more of scrambled eggs and bacon," Albright replied. "Perhaps some toast and a cup of coffee."

Len thought the old man was crazy. "Sorry, Dr. Albright. We don't have anything like that."

The smile suddenly left the doctor's face. "Len, it is obvious to me that you and Miles are more advanced than Kirkland and the others—intellectually I mean."

"I wouldn't say that."

"We must admit the truth, young man. I'll need you and Miles to help me, but I have to know that I can trust you. We must work as a team if we are going to get out of this alive."

"You saved Miles," Len replied. "You stood up to Kirkland and the others. That's good enough for me."

"You are a very wise young man."

Albright took another look at Miles. The boy's chest was rising and falling in a regular rhythm. "The serum could not have worked better," he said softly.

Albright moved away from his patient and looked at Len. "Very well. If I am going to take you into my confidence, then we must start right away."

"I don't understand."

"You will, Len."

Albright walked to the wall on the other side of the room and ran his hand along the doorjamb. When he hit a secret button, another piece of the wall began to slide.

Len's eyes were wide. "How did you—"

"I designed this laboratory," Albright said. "You discovered only the tip of the iceberg when you opened the other wall. How did you discover the password?"

"By accident," Len replied.

Albright gestured to the opening. "After you, Mr. Hayden."

Len hesitated. "What's in there?"

"It's only an elevator," the doctor replied. "If you'll join me, we'll have breakfast within the hour."

Albright stepped inside the tiny boxlike chamber.

Len had decided to trust Albright. He had not let him down so far. He got in beside him.

Albright pressed a button, and the elevator began to descend.

They seemed to be falling through the rock of the earth. When the elevator finally stopped, Len heard the echoes of lapping water.

Albright stepped out onto a narrow wooden pier that ringed a hidden grotto. "We have arrived."

As he moved onto the pier, Len surveyed the grotto. Moored to the pier was a long, well-lit ship at least fifty feet in length. It rocked slightly in the motion of the water.

Len silently read the name of their salvation: *"Proteus."*

Kirkland opened his eyes and stared at the stone wall of the upper laboratory. Streaks of sunlight bounced off the wall, forcing him to close his eyes for a moment. His head still ached from the doctor's jolt.

Sitting up slowly, Kirkland tried to remember what had happened. He recalled the doctor's pointed face and gray eyes—and the great pain that had knocked him out.

"Hey, both of you! Wake up!"

Cruiser and D.J. were startled into consciousness. They sat up on the floor where they had slept all night.

Cruiser's eyes widened when he saw Kirkland. "We thought you were dead! That doctor shot you with the stun-gun!"

Kirkland gazed toward the aluminum gate that sealed off the basement below. "He's down there with Len and Miles. He knocked me out twice in one day."

"He did save us from the mutants," D.J. offered.

Kirkland stood up slowly on wobbly legs. "We have to find a way to get in there. He's got the boat—and we're going to get it, even if we have to kill him!"

Len carried a silver tray across the pier toward the elevator. His head was spinning with visions of the fantastic *Proteus*. It was the most unusual water craft he had ever seen. It even rivaled the nuclear sub that Len had seen in the navy yard at Portsmouth, New Hampshire.

Stepping into the elevator, Len pushed the red button. His spirits soared as it ascended. Dr. Albright had been a good host. He had served eggs for breakfast and even made up a tray for Miles. The *Proteus* was equipped with living quarters that included a full galley. They were going to move Miles as soon as he was able to walk.

The elevator stopped, and Len stepped into the lab basement. Miles was still sleeping. Len put the tray on the stool next to the padded table.

"Bookman," Len said quietly, "wake up. Wait till you see the doctor's ship. It's unbelievable! We're almost out of here."

Miles stirred to life. "Hayden?"

Len gestured to the tray. "Here, sit up a little. You can eat some soup. The doctor said it's all right."

He started to lift Miles's head, but the boy sat up suddenly and threw his legs over the table.

Len stepped back, gaping. Miles had not even winced when he sat up.

"Bookman, what's with you?"

Miles ran a hand through his hair. "I feel better. That soup smells good. I'm hungry!"

Miles hopped off the table. He grabbed the soup bowl and lifted it to his mouth. He slurped the broth directly from the bowl.

"Unreal," Len said under his breath.

Miles looked sideways at him. "What's wrong, Hayden? Your face is white."

Len looked at the wound on Miles's torso. The incision was a dull pink. It looked almost healed. He shook his head. "Bookman, yesterday I had you figured for a coffin. Today you're walking. It's weird."

A concerned look formed on Miles's face. "I wonder what that doctor did to me. I feel great."

"No pain?"

"The incision itches a little, but I feel better than ever."

"Remarkable," a voice said from across the room.

Albright was in front of the elevator. They had not heard him arrive. His face lit up in surprise when he saw Miles. He had not expected to see Miles walking around so soon after the operation, either.

"Remarkable," the doctor said again in wonderment. "All my years of research have not

71

been in vain. My colleagues will no longer call me insane. I must record this in my journal at once."

Albright pulled a small notebook from his coat and began to scribble, whispering to himself. Len and Miles exchanged a cautious glance.

Miles touched his side where the arrow had gone in. He felt only a dull sensation. "Doctor, what did you do to me?"

Albright folded up the notebook and put it back in his pocket. "I saved your life, Miles."

"But how?"

"By injecting you with a formula of my own creation. It is, for lack of a better phrase, a supervitamin mixture. Completely organic. It restored your tissues overnight. You may still feel some residual pain, but you will be back to normal in a few days."

A strange smile appeared on Miles's face. "It's a miracle. Maybe the biggest breakthrough in scientific history. Doctor, you'll take your place beside Pasteur and Salk."

Albright stiffened proudly. "It will cure almost any bacterial infection within forty-eight hours. I'm also working on a viral formula."

"That would mean a cure for cancer," Miles said with enthusiasm.

Len squinted at the doctor. "A medicine that cures anything in a couple of days?"

Albright gestured to Miles. "Observe the results yourself. Have you forgotten how badly your friend was hurt? He is back from the dead. I helped him cheat death."

Miles perceived a strange gleam in the doctor's eyes. "Doctor, I appreciate your help. But I think I should warn you. On an island south of here—"

"I know all about them," Albright said, lowering his head. "That's why I have returned. I want to use my serum on those lost souls. If I can reverse the effects of my earlier experiments, perhaps they will have a chance to live like human beings. Even they deserve that fate."

Len grimaced. "Doc, these guys are—"

Albright waved him off. "We will discuss this later. Right now, I want to show Miles the *Proteus*."

Len hesitated.

Miles shook his head. "Humor him, Hayden. He's our ticket out of here," he whispered.

Reluctantly, Len joined Miles and Albright in the elevator. When they emerged into the grotto, Miles stopped to appreciate the vessel.

Albright led them over the gangplank. He began the tour in the aft section. Pointing to the radar unit, he explained the technical side of the rescue in which he had easily snatched Kirkland, Cruiser, and D.J. from the jaws of the bandits. Then he showed them the mortar tubes that he used to fire the smoke bombs.

Taking them forward, he showed Miles the control center of the ship. The entire vessel could be run from one computer keyboard on the bridge. Cameras were mounted on all sides of the ship, relaying the images to a panel of monitors over the control panel. The captain had a good view in any direction.

Albright sat down behind the flashing keyboard. "I can interface with the security system in the laboratory. Here, let's see if all the circuits are still working."

He punched a yellow button marked UPPER LAB. Suddenly, three boys appeared on one of the monitors. Kirkland was pacing back and forth. Cruiser and D.J. were sitting on the floor. Kirkland turned quickly and threw something at the aluminum gate that blocked the stairs.

"Like an animal in a cage," Albright muttered.

Miles frowned at the monitor. A spell of weakness came over him, and he had to sit down for a moment.

"Water," he said, "please."

They led him downstairs to the galley. Miles felt better after he drank, but small beads of sweat broke out on his face.

Albright sat down with the boys at the galley table. "You are fine young men. Well educated, intelligent, brave. I want to assure you that I intend to return you to your homes safely."

Len smiled. "We're ready to go, sir."

"The sooner the better," Miles said.

Albright leaned back, frowning. "I'm afraid we must stay here awhile longer. I want to test my serum on the men who suffered from my experiments. I want to see if it can reverse the damage."

Len's face flushed red with anger. "Wait just a minute! We can't go after Meat Hook. He's too dangerous."

"We can use the *Proteus*," Albright replied. "I have gas bombs to put them to sleep. I can inoculate them while they're out. It will be no trouble at all. You two could help me give the injections."

"Take us home first. Then you can come back here and do whatever you want," Len said.

"I cannot leave until my work is finished," the doctor replied sadly. "I stole this vessel from the navy yard in San Diego. When the authorities find me, I will be arrested. No, I have to inoculate those men before we leave. It's the only way."

"You're crazy!" Len shouted. "We can't go after Meat Hook, even if we do have this boat."

Miles's face grew hopeful. "Maybe we don't have to go after Meat Hook. There might be another way."

Albright glanced sideways at Miles. "What's on your mind, Miles?"

Miles leaned forward. "If you could test your serum on one of the bandits, would that be good enough for you?"

Albright shrugged. "Possibly."

Miles snapped his fingers. "There's a mutant right here on this island—the guy who shot me with his crossbow."

"Really?" the doctor asked.

"We could catch him," Miles went on. "You could try the serum on him. If it works, we could send him back to the island with serum for the others. It would give them a choice."

"I'm not sure that would work," Albright replied, "but it would be good to have a test subject here in the lab."

"It makes sense," Miles said. "You could run a controlled experiment. If the serum doesn't work, we can leave without having to face the mutants."

Albright smiled. "You are a very bright young man, Miles."

"Bright?" Len said. "He's crazy. We could never run down that wild man."

Miles looked straight into the doctor's gray eyes. "If we delivered you a subject for the experiment, Dr. Albright, would you promise to take us back to civilization after you test your formula on him?"

Albright considered the boy's proposal. "I could help you from the ship. The island is loaded with hidden security devices. I could even interface and help you track the man. But I'm afraid Len is right. You two could never capture a dangerous criminal by yourselves. The peril would be too great."

Miles sighed and pointed to the monitor. "Kirkland and the others can help us."

Len shook his head. "They wouldn't help us."

Miles held up his finger. "If we told them we're going home after the experiment, they'd listen to reason."

Albright rubbed his pointed chin. "I don't know—"

"We can do it," Miles said. "I know we can."

"Who's going to talk to Kirkland?" Len asked.

Miles took a deep breath. "I will."

Albright shrugged. "Very well, Miles. Find the subject for my experiment, and I will gladly take you off this cursed island."

Kirkland was leaning back against the aluminum gate when it started to open. He jumped across the room and almost lost his balance.

The gate stopped at the ceiling. A lone figure was coming up the stairs. At first, Kirkland could not see the face in the shadows. Then the boy walked under the gate, taking a step into the light.

"Bookman, you're alive."

Miles stood straight, keeping calm. "The doctor saved me, Kirkland. He performed an oper—"

Kirkland picked up a wooden chair and smashed it on the floor, grabbing a chair leg to use as a club. He was ready to attack.

"Listen to me," Miles pleaded. "The doctor is going to help us."

Kirkland took a few steps toward the stairs. "Get outta my way, prep. I'm going to smash in that doctor's crummy head."

Miles lifted the stun-gun, which had been in his hand all the time. "One more step, Kirkland, and I throw the switch on you."

Kirkland's dark eyes widened at the sight of the electric weapon. He recalled the first shock and backed away, dropping the club to the lab floor.

"Okay, prep. I'm cool."

Cruiser and D.J. also shrank away from the stun-gun. Miles kept it pointed at them.

"Albright needs our help," Miles told them. "If we cooperate, he'll take us back to civilization."

"Right!" Cruiser said skeptically. "We can't trust him, Bookman."

"He cured me," Miles replied. "Isn't that proof that he doesn't mean to hurt us?"

D.J. nodded dumbly.

"It's a trick," Cruiser said. "Miles is in on it with the doctor."

Miles grimaced, shaking his head. "You really are as stupid as you look, Cruiser."

"You're the stupid one!" Cruiser replied.

"I'm the one with the gun," Miles said. "Kirkland?"

"All right, I'm listening. What does the old guy want?" Kirkland asked.

"Dr. Albright was the head of the research project on this island," Miles explained. "His experiments resulted in Meat Hook and the rest of that horror show to the south."

"And you're ready to trust somebody like that?" Kirkland scoffed.

Miles's eyes narrowed on the older boy. "I'd trust him before I'd trust you. You left me to die, Kirkland. The doctor saved my life. Who would you trust if you were me?"

Kirkland shifted on his feet nervously. "Nothing personal, Bookman. I was going to send someone back for you."

"Maybe we ought to leave your worthless butt out here. Forget about our offer," Miles said.

"Wait!" Kirkland cried. "Okay, what does the doctor want?"

Miles sighed. "He has a new serum. He wants to test it on one of Meat Hook's goons. It might make them human again if it works."

Kirkland shook his head. "No way. I'm not going back to that island."

Miles chortled in dismay. "Use your brain,

Kirkland. There's a mutant right here on this island, the one who shot me."

"You're right," Kirkland said.

"If we catch him," Miles offered, "the doctor will try his serum. Then he will take us back to Hawaii."

Kirkland waved his hand. "Wait a minute. What if this stuff doesn't work?"

Miles shrugged. "Either way, we're out of here."

"If it *does* work, what'll happen?" Cruiser asked.

"The army can come back and mop up," Miles replied. "The authorities can inoculate Meat Hook's gang. I'm telling you, this is our ticket out. You idiots can blow it if you want, but I'm helping the doctor."

D.J. stepped forward a little. "Why don't we vote on it?"

Kirkland shook his head. "No good. It'd be a standoff."

"No it wouldn't, Kirkland. I'm voting with Miles."

They all turned. Augie was standing with Commando in the doorway of the lab.

"I vote with Miles," Augie said again. "So does Commando."

Kirkland scowled. "That mutt can't vote."

Augie gestured toward Kirkland. "Commando!"

The wild-looking dog shot across the room and knocked Kirkland to the floor. Commando pinned his shoulders with his paws. White teeth were inches from Kirkland's throat.

"Okay!" Kirkland shouted. "Get this beast off me!"

Augie grinned at Miles, ignoring Kirkland. "Wow—I thought you were a goner."

"The doctor saved me," Miles replied. "Come on, Augie. Come stay with us on the ship."

"Ship!" Kirkland yelled.

Commando left his shoulders, but Kirkland was too late. While he was still scurrying to his feet, Augie and Commando followed Miles under the gate and it dropped quickly to the floor, sealing off the lower lab again.

Kirkland ran to the gate, banging his fists in rage. "Let us in. You hear me? Let us in!"

Albright's calm voice suddenly filled the room. "You must learn to control your temper, Mr. Kirkland. There's no need to shout. I can see and hear you."

Kirkland wheeled around. "Where are you, old man? Show yourself. I'll fight you right here."

"Don't worry," the voice said over the speaker. "Food and water will be provided for you as long as you help me. After my experiments are completed, you will all be returned safely to the mainland."

81

"If you double-cross us, I'll kill you!" Kirkland shouted. "Do you hear me? I'll kill you!"

But the speaker was silent. Kirkland and the others would have to wait until the doctor wanted their attention again. As long as they were on the island, they would be at the mercy of the doctor.

"Hayden, check this out."

Miles sat behind the control panel of the *Proteus* computer. His fingers moved rapidly over the keyboard. After two days of Albright's tutelage, he had mastered the intricacies of the ship's software.

Len stared at the multicolored lights of the panel. "What are you doing?"

"This."

Miles hit a red button, and a holograph formed in the air in front of them. It was a map of the island. Miles brought up a green grid on the map. He isolated the position of the compound with a red dot.

"We're right here," he told Len. "Watch this. I can interface with compound security."

He typed the command on the keyboard. Bright blue dots formed in a semicircle around the red one. Len shook his head. Something felt wrong.

"The blue dots are security listening devices," Miles said.

"Bugs," Len replied. "The doctor likes to spy on people."

"We can hear what's going on inside the compound and within a half-mile radius of the grounds. Listen."

His fingers flashed across the keyboard. Suddenly, the voices of Cruiser and Kirkland filled the cabin. They were arguing. Cruiser wanted to go along with the doctor's plan, but Kirkland wanted to smash Albright's head in.

"Pleasant conversation," Miles said.

Len squinted at his friend. Miles didn't seem any different from before. The too-quick recovery scared Len. It was eerie.

Miles hit the keys again. "We can listen to the jungle."

The cries of squawking birds came over the speakers. Miles was about to give the computer another command when he heard a loud crash in the rain forest. Grunts and cursing followed the noise.

Miles looked at the grid. "I've got to pinpoint this."

He worked on the keyboard until a yellow dot appeared on the grid. The noises were coming from below the compound, at the edge of the jungle.

"He's close," Miles said excitedly. "I should call the doctor. He'll want to see this." He reached for a phone receiver.

Len grabbed his wrist. "No."

"Hayden, what's your problem?"

"This isn't a game," Len replied. "The doctor gave you that serum."

"So? It cured me, didn't it?"

"The mutants," Len whispered. "Albright gave them a serum once. Look what happened to—"

The cabin door opened, and Albright stepped in. Len grew quiet.

"I think I found something," Miles said. "I keyed in the audio response and isolated some strange sounds on the grid. Listen."

Miles turned up the volume. An inhuman cry echoed from the jungle. They could hear the trees shaking.

"He's close," Miles said. "We could take him now."

Albright smiled. "Good work, Miles. You have learned well. It is time to finish our work. Alert the others. Len, you come with me."


Kirkland looked up when the aluminum gate began to slide. He rushed toward the gate, but he was not fast enough. A large box came through the opening, then the gate slammed down, almost crushing the tips of his fingers.

Kirkland kicked the box. Cruiser and D.J. opened it up. They were expecting their daily ration of food and water, but they found a surprise.

Kirkland pulled out a walkie-talkie and a pistol.

A voice came over the walkie-talkie. "It's a tranquilizer pistol," Miles said. "You've only got one shot, Kirkland. Make it count."

"I'll use it on *you!*" Kirkland shouted.

"Forget it," Miles replied. "It's showtime. Are you Neanderthals ready to go?"

Kirkland scowled at the walls, looking for the camera. "Shut up!"

"Don't blow it," Miles replied in a condescending tone. "This is your last chance to get out of here, Kirkland. Otherwise, we visit Uncle Meat Hook and put you in a cage."

"Just shut up!" Kirkland shouted, waving the tranquilizer pistol.

"I'm not going to talk to you until you are civil."

Kirkland managed to control himself. "Okay, okay." Anything was better than Meat Hook's cages.

"Leave the building. Once you get outside, listen to the radio. I'll tell you what to do."

"All right. I'm going."

"Good," Miles replied. "Let's catch ourselves a mutant."

* * *

After they had pushed the box into the upper lab, Len waited on the stairs for Albright. The doctor went into the Proteus room and returned with a large leather case. As he came back up the stairs, he paused to catch his breath.

"Are you all right?" Len asked.

The doctor nodded.

"I haven't seen Augie this morning," Len said. "Where is he?"

"He went out earlier," Albright replied. "The dog had to hunt."

Len winced. "I hope they don't get in the way."

The doctor handed him the leather case. "Here. Your tools."

Len found a walkie-talkie and a pair of high-powered binoculars. "What are these for?"

"Do you know your way up the mountain?" the doctor asked. "To the ledge in front of the storage area?"

"The cave," Len replied. "Yes, I know it."

Albright motioned toward the aluminum gate. "Climb to the ledge."

"Why?"

"I want you to act as a spotter," Albright replied. "You will be more versatile than any television camera."

Len hesitated. "What about Kirkland and the others? They'll waste me if I run into them."

"They are operating below, in the jungle.

When you see that they have captured their quarry, hurry back here. I will see to it that you are safe."

Albright opened the gate. Len hesitated.

"You don't have to go if you don't want to," Albright said. "I'll understand."

"No, I'll go."

Len ducked under the gate. He had survived too long to let anything stop him from getting off the island.

He left the lab and started up the mountain trail.

An hour later, Miles's voice came over the walkie-talkie. "Home base to mutant patrol. What's happening out there?"

Len pressed the button of his radio. "Nothing so far," he said into the receiver. "I can see Kirkland and the others, but that's it."

From his vantage point on the mountain, Len studied the jungle with the high-powered binoculars. They had not seen Dog Face yet, but they knew he was somewhere near the compound. The instruments in the *Proteus* did not lie.

Miles's voice came over the speaker again. "Kirkland, do you see anything yet?"

No response from the jungle.

"Kirkland?"

The gruff reply finally came over the airwaves. "What do you want?"

87

"See anything?"

"No," Kirkland replied. "You're crazy, Bookman. There's nothing out here."

"Keep looking," Miles said.

"Yeah, right."

Len continued to scan the thick growth with the binoculars. He saw birds flitting between the flowered vines. The sun baked the ceiling of the forest, causing steam to rise into the air.

Then Len caught sight of movement in the treetops. Something shook the vines. Suddenly, an ugly face loomed out at him from the greenery.

"I've spotted him," Len said over the radio. "He's just below the compound. Kirkland, he's close to you. Real close."

But Kirkland didn't acknowledge the warning. Len saw them moving through the jungle. When he focused the binoculars on the mutant again, the ugly face was gone.

"I can't find him," Len said. "He's disappeared."

Miles sounded urgent over the walkie-talkie. "Be careful, Kirkland. Kirkland?"

There was no reply. Kirkland had switched off his walkie-talkie. Miles could no longer help them.

Kirkland grunted as he pushed through the tangle of vines. He didn't believe there was anyone in the jungle and he wasn't going to let Miles tell him what to do. That was why he had turned off the radio.

Cruiser and D.J. were trudging behind him. They too were ready to give up the chase. The jungle was hot, and they had seen no sign of the mutant.

Kirkland stopped for a moment. "Give it a rest."

Cruiser moaned, leaning back against a tree.

"I hate this!" D.J. whined.

Kirkland peered into the shadows of the rain forest. "Just a few more minutes, then we'll get out of here. I'm going after the doctor."

After they had rested, Kirkland started forward again. Cruiser followed on the trail, but D.J. hung back, straggling. He was ready to collapse in the heat.

"Hey, wait up."

Kirkland looked over his shoulder. His eyes grew wide. A crashing noise resounded in the trees, and something fell on top of D.J.

"The mutant!" Kirkland cried.

A hideous face leered up at them. D.J. was unconscious. Dog Face wrapped his crusty fingers around D.J.'s neck.

Miles was growing impatient in the control room of the *Proteus*. "Hayden, what's going on out there?"

Len was scanning the green ceiling with the binoculars. "I can't see a thing, Miles. I lost them."

Miles sighed. "Kirkland turned off his radio. What an idiot. I'm going to try the sound devices."

"Come on, Kirkland!" Len muttered under his breath.

"Hayden? I think the mutant trashed the microphone in that sector."

Len looked through the glasses again, holding them with one hand. "I don't see any—wait a minute."

There was some movement in the trees again. Len caught flashes of white. Then the movement was gone, and the jungle was quiet.

Kirkland raised the tranquilizer gun at Dog Face, but he could not take aim. His hand was shaking.

"He's going to kill D.J.!" Cruiser cried.

Kirkland lowered the weapon. He could not fire without hitting D.J.

"Kirkland!"

Dog Face seemed to be laughing at them. Kirkland had to shoot. He had to take him out before he killed D.J.

Kirkland looked down the barrel of the gun. His finger tightened on the trigger, but he didn't fire. Something brushed past him and caused him to lose his balance.

A wild animal leaped onto the mutant. Dog Face rolled off D.J. Both of them snarled as they began to fight.

"Commando!" Cruiser cried.

Kirkland pointed the pistol again.

"No!" Augie stepped in front of him. "You might hit my dog!"

Commando yelped as the mutant pushed him aside. Dog Face stood up, snarling at Kirkland. Kirkland pulled the trigger of the tranquilizer pistol.

The dart lodged in Dog Face's chest. Dog Face stared in disbelief at the needle in his body. He started to reach for the dart, but he was unable to grab it. The tranquilizer kicked in and knocked him to the jungle floor. The boys stood for a moment, afraid to approach him.

Augie clapped his hands. "Commando! Good boy, Commando!" The dog curled around his legs like a puppy.

Kirkland glared at Augie. "Where'd you come from?"

Augie shrugged. "We were hunting."

Kirkland sighed. "Help us drag this monster back to the compound. The doctor wants to see him."

Augie moved away. "I'm not going with you."

Cruiser grabbed his arm. "Where do you think you're going?"

Commando bared his teeth at Cruiser who quickly let go of Augie. Augie kept moving. "I go where I want, Cruiser. I'm leaving."

He disappeared into the jungle with the dog close behind.

"I'm gonna eat that dog for breakfast one day," Cruiser muttered.

Kirkland nodded toward D.J. "Let's see if he's all right."

They managed to bring D.J. around. His neck was sore, but he was all right. He stood up and looked at their captive.

"Come on, we've got to get him back to the lab," Kirkland said.

Cruiser pointed to the walkie-talkie. "Aren't you going to call Miles?"

Kirkland shook his head, smiling a little. "No. I've got a surprise for the doctor."

Miles's voice came over the radio. "Hayden? Anything?"

Len lowered the binoculars and lifted the walkie-talkie. "Negative."

"Hold on. Dr. Albright wants to speak to you."

The doctor's voice crackled through the receiver. "Come down from the mountain, Len. You've been up there long enough."

"I'm on my way," Len replied.

The descent took the better part of an hour. When Len was almost to the compound, he stopped dead on the trail.

Kirkland and the others were moving toward the lab, dragging the limp body of Dog Face across the plateau. Len ducked into the brush so they wouldn't see him.

He raised the walkie-talkie. "Bookman. Bookman, come in," he whispered.

"Right here," Miles replied.

"They're here," Len told him. "They've got the mutant."

"Hold on."

Dr. Albright's voice came on. "Stay where you are, Len. And be quiet so the others don't hear you."

The radio went dead. Len peered through the undergrowth and watched the boys enter the lab building.

They dropped Dog Face in front of the aluminum gate. "Okay, Doctor, we delivered. Now, come on out and face us."

Albright's voice filled the upper lab. "Thank you, Mr. Kirkland. You've done well."

"Show yourself, Albright. We did what you wanted. Now you've got to keep your end of the deal."

"I intend to honor our bargain," Albright replied. "But you must first allow me to complete my experiments."

Kirkland shook his head. "Forget it. We got the mutant. You deal with us."

"You will all be taken home," Albright promised. "But you must allow me to complete my work."

Kirkland picked up a piece of wood and threatened Dog Face. "Let us in, Doc, or I'll cave in his skull. I swear I'll do it."

After a pause, Albright said, "Very well. Have it your own way. I'll do what you ask, but don't kill him."

Kirkland smiled triumphantly. He waited for the gate to open, his right hand clutching the hunk of wood. He planned to crush Albright's skull as soon as the gate went up. He could not smell the odorless gas that seeped into the upper lab through the air vents. In a few moments, Kirkland and the others were lying unconscious on the floor beside Dog Face.

"Okay," Miles said over the walkie-talkie. "You can come down, Hayden."

Len pushed the talk button. "Are you sure?"

"Kirkland and company are taken care of. They won't give you any more trouble."

"I'm on my way."

Len trod down the narrow path. Cautiously, he approached the lab building. When he looked through the door, he saw Dr. Albright bending over the body of Dog Face and the boys passed out on the floor.

"Are they dead?" Len asked.

"It's a harmless gas," Albright replied. "It will wear off in a couple of hours. They'll be fine."

They dragged Dog Face through the aluminum gates. Len held the mutant while Albright pushed a box of food into the upper lab. Albright said the password, and the gate closed again.

When the doctor turned back toward Len, he smiled warmly. "Don't look so glum, my young friend. You're almost home."

Len just nodded. "Sure."

They dragged the body into the basement. Miles, who had come up from the ship, helped them lift Dog Face onto the padded table.

As Albright strapped his patient to the table, Len and Miles stared down at the twisted face. The features were swollen and distorted. Len wondered if Miles would soon look the same way.

"What's wrong?" Miles asked.

Len shook his head. "Nothing. He just looks weird."

Albright was already filling the hypodermic needle. "We shall see if we can remedy the ills of this unfortunate soul."

The doctor injected his serum into the patient. Len stepped back a little, while Miles looked on with detached curiosity. He bore no malice toward the bandit who had wounded him.

When the serum kicked in, Dog Face's body stiffened and went into convulsions.

"Do something!" Len pleaded.

The doctor shook his head slowly. "I've done all I can."

After a few minutes, the mutant stopped twitching, his body limp. Len looked closely to see if the creature had died. The chest rose and fell slowly. The doctor had not killed him—yet.

They spent the rest of the day observing the patient. Dog Face awoke only once, thrashing and growling as he fought to get out of his bonds. But the straps held, and he passed out again. Albright injected a tranquilizer to make sure he slept for a while.

Miles had also grown quiet and withdrawn. Would there be aftereffects from the serum that had cured him?

Albright was exhausted. "I'm going below to the ship. Please notify me if there are any changes."

Miles nodded.

Albright walked to the elevator. He smiled, then descended to the *Proteus* to rest.

As soon as they were alone, Len turned to Miles. "This is weird, Bookman."

"I know," Miles replied. "The serum doesn't seem to be working on him."

"It worked on you. Do you feel any different?"

Miles shook his head. "No, I feel great."

Len stared at Dog Face. "I hope you don't end up like him."

"I hope I don't end up like him either."


Len opened his eyes, waking from a dreamless slumber in the lab. Albright had assigned him the late watch. He had stayed with the patient all night, but there had been no significant developments.

Len rose and stretched to work out the kinks. He walked over to the table and looked down at Dog Face.

Len's jaw dropped, and he jumped back from the table. The patient's eyes were wide open. Clear blue irises stared back at Len. The creature on the table did something that Len never would have expected—he smiled.

"Hello," the patient said in a calm voice. "Have you got a cigarette?"

Len rubbed his eyes. It had to be a dream. The mutant was responding to him like a human being!

"Are you all right?" the patient asked him.

"Unbelievable!" Len muttered. "You're talking!"

"Where am I? Is this prison?"

**97**

"Sort of," Len replied. "Don't you remember?"

"Sometimes I forget," the patient replied. "Don't you have a cigarette? I'm dying for one."

Len reached for the intercom button. "Anybody awake down there?"

Miles answered the call. "What's up, Hayden?"

"Get up here now," Len replied. "Bring the doctor."

"Why?"

"The mutant's awake, Bookman. Only he's not a mutant anymore."

Dr. Albright bent over the padded table. "Good morning, sir. What's your name?"

"Stanley," the patient replied calmly. "Stanley Johnson."

Albright nodded. "Good. Memory intact— he's aware of who he is. Tell me about yourself, Stanley."

The patient sighed, rolling his eyes. "I killed my mother and father with a hatchet. I'm doing life in San Quentin."

"Do you remember coming to the South Seas?" Albright asked.

"The South Seas? Isn't this San Quentin?"

"You see," the doctor said to Miles and Len. "My serum restored his memory of life before our experiments. Look, the face isn't as puffy as it was. He resembles a human."

"Hey," the patient said, "I resent that! I'm a human. I made a few mistakes, but I'm okay."

"Of course you are," Albright replied. "Of course you are."

Miles breathed more easily. "I guess this means I'm going to be all right."

Albright smiled. "There was never any doubt."

Len felt a little better. "It really worked! Look at him."

"Would you like to come with me, Stanley?" the doctor asked.

"Where are we going?"

"To have some breakfast," Albright replied. "We must find you some clothes. I'd like to examine you—take some blood samples."

"Okay," the patient said. "Let me off this table."

"I'll have to cuff your hands and ankles," Albright replied. "You won't mind, will you, Stanley?"

The patient shrugged. "I'm used to it. I promise I won't cause any trouble. Just let me off."

But Albright was taking no chances. He rummaged through the lab drawers until he found handcuffs and the leg irons. When Stanley was sufficiently restrained, Albright released the straps that held him to the table.

Stanley sat up quickly. Len and Miles stepped back a little, but the former bandit made no threatening moves. Instead, he hopped off the table and smiled at Albright.

"I'm ready," he said in a friendly tone.

Albright took his arm, leading Stanley toward the elevator. "Len, Miles—shall we go?"

Len shook his head. "I'll stay here."

Miles started for the elevator. "Hold down the fort, Hayden. I'll be back in a while with some breakfast."

The three of them climbed into the elevator. Len sat down against the wall.

After an hour, Miles returned to the lab with a tray of eggs and toast. Len, suddenly ravenous, wolfed down the food.

"Stanley is as meek as a kitten," Miles said. "A regular honor student. That serum did the trick."

Len nodded between bites. Some of his fears were vanishing.

"We'll be out of here soon," Miles went on. "Wait till Old Man Hauck hears about what we did on our summer vacation. That's one English composition he'll read out loud in class."

Suddenly an alarm sounded. The lights flashed, then went out. They were sitting in the darkness.

"What happened?" Len asked.

Miles pressed the intercom button, which ran off the batteries in the *Proteus*. "Dr. Albright?"

There was no reply.

"The mutant!" Len said. "He got the doctor!"

But then they heard the aluminum gate sliding up. Footsteps resounded in the stairwell. The electricity flashed on again, but it was too late. Kirkland and the others were already inside the basement.

# Eight

Kirkland glared at Len and Miles. "Payback time!" He rushed toward Miles, swinging his right hand.

Miles ducked the blow, but the hard right caught Len in the mouth. Len went down with blood flowing between his lips.

Kirkland swung at Miles again. Miles avoided the blow. Kirkland kept coming, but Miles was too quick. Kirkland couldn't lay a hand on him.

"Stand still, you little creep!"

"Leave us alone," Miles said. "If you blow it for us, Kirkland, we'll never get off this island."

Kirkland lunged at him. Miles side-stepped the attack again. He backed away, keeping his eyes on the dark-haired delinquent.

"Give it up, Kirkland. You can't beat the doctor."

Miles ran to the wall, pressing the intercom

button. "Dr. Albright, help us. They got through the door."

But there was no reply. The electrical outage had probably shorted the intercom system. Miles turned to see all three of them coming at him.

"You'll never get away with his," he told them. "The doctor will fix you when he—"

"Shut up!" Kirkland cried. "Cruiser, D.J.— grab him."

The two boys closed in on Miles, seizing his arms.

"Where's the doctor?" Kirkland demanded.

"I won't tell you," Miles replied.

Cruiser put a piece of jagged metal to Miles's throat. "Tell us, punk, or I'll open you up."

Len staggered to his feet. "The elevator," he said to Kirkland. "It leads to a cave down below."

Kirkland glared at Len. "Where's the elevator?"

Len showed him the button and he opened the door.

"Get in the elevator," Kirkland snarled at Len, "or Miles is dead."

Miles sighed. "Guys like you never learn."

They crowded into the elevator. It was barely big enough to hold all of them. Kirkland pressed the button and the elevator whirred, descending through the rock.

"He's gonna take us off this island just like he promised," Kirkland said, "or we kill Miles."

Len stared at the jagged metal, but Miles did not seem to be afraid. He trusted the doctor.

The elevator finally stopped. When the door opened, the boys stepped out onto the narrow pier. Len's eyes grew wide, and Miles frowned.

Kirkland let out a hostile cry.

They stared at the empty slip. Water lapped against the pilings. Dr. Albright and the *Proteus* were gone.

Kirkland stood on the end of the pier, staring out at the mouth of the grotto. "I knew I shouldn't have trusted him."

"What are we going to do now?" Cruiser asked.

Len looked at Miles, who shook his head. Miles leaned back against the wall of rock that abutted the pier. His arms were folded over his chest, and his expression was disinterested.

Kirkland wheeled around to glare at him. "You, Bookman! You're responsible for this."

Miles sighed, shaking his head. "In case you haven't noticed, Kirkland, Len and I were left behind just like you."

Kirkland couldn't argue with the facts. He made a growling noise and stomped his foot against the pier.

"All right, Bookman," he said finally. "Where did Albright go?"

Miles shrugged. "How should I know?"

Kirkland got up in his face. "Because you know everything! At least you think you do! Where'd he go?"

"He's gone to the other island," Len replied. "He's going to try his serum on the mutants."

"Bull!" Kirkland cried.

"The serum turned Dog Face into a human being," Miles said. "He should have tried it on you."

Kirkland glowered at Miles, but he did not attack. He looked out toward the mouth of the cave. The sun glistened on the blue water beyond the grotto.

"He won't come back," Kirkland said. "Come on, Cruiser, D.J. Let's go upstairs and find something to eat. I got to figure out our next move."

Len started for the elevator.

Kirkland stopped him. "No way, Hayden. You and your genius friend stay here in case he does come back."

"Wait," Len protested.

Miles waved him off. "Forget it, Hayden. You might as well argue with a brick wall. Go on, Kirkland. We'll stay."

Kirkland glared at Miles before he stepped back into the elevator. Cruiser and D.J. followed him and the door closed.

Miles immediately turned toward the wall of rock. "I thought they'd never leave." He began to feel along the rock face with his fingers.

Len squinted at his friend. "What are you doing?"

"I found some information in the computer files," Miles replied. "The doctor had a lot of little secrets that he never told us. He—wait a minute, I think I found it."

Miles lifted a flap of loose rock. Behind the flap was a red switch. Miles flipped the switch and the rock began to move at the end of the pier.

Len stared in amazement as the opening grew larger.

They walked to the end of the pier and looked into the hidden cave. Water rushed in from the grotto, floating a speed boat that was moored inside the compartment. The boat bobbed in the tide.

"Bookman, what did—hey!"

Miles had jumped into the water. He swam to the boat and pulled himself over the side. The battery was dead, so it took him several minutes to pull-start the huge outboard engine. When it finally roared to life, he untied the lines and eased toward the end of the pier.

Len hopped into the idling vessel. Miles put it in gear and guided the boat into the chop of the open sea.

Miles shook his head. "Bummer."

"What?" Len asked.

Miles pointed to the fuel gauge on the gas tank. "We're low on gas. Only half a tank."

Len frowned. "That won't get us to Hawaii."

Miles looked to the south. "I say we chase the *Proteus.*"

Len also gazed toward Lost Island. "Do you really think Albright went back to the mutant camp?"

"Where else?" Miles replied. "When he left, the power went off for a minute. That was when Kirkland and crew were able to sneak in. He had been running the lab on the boat's generator. I guess the other generator kicked in when he decided to run. He's going to test his serum. And we have to find him. It's our only chance."

Miles turned the boat to the south. "It's twenty miles to the island, give or take five miles. If we go at two or three miles an hour, we'd save gas. We'd make it after dark."

"After dark?"

Miles looked at his friend. "Do you want Meat Hook and his men to see us?"

"Good point," Len replied. "All right, Bookman. Let's do it."

They started slowly to the south, making for Lost Island.

# Nine

Vinnie Pelligrino stared down through the bamboo bars at the bandit encampment. Meat Hook and his men had been busy. The huge platform was finished. Several bandits moved about the camp, lighting torches to ward off the first shadows of evening. They were making preparations for a ceremony on the beach.

Vinnie touched his throat. He knew he was going to be the sacrificial lamb. They would chop off his head, as they had done to Joey Wolfe. Cannibal would drag him into the jungle.

"My, my. We are pensive tonight."

Vinnie looked down at Cannibal. The clown-ish, hollow face reflected in the torchlight as he stirred his caldron.

Cannibal laughed. "Tonight you will become one with us, Carrot-Top. Meat Hook has special plans for you."

"What kind of plans?" Vinnie asked.

"You will take your place among the immortals."

Vinnie watched as some of the workers came to a sudden halt. Their faces were turned toward the lagoon.

A messenger came running up the beach to Meat Hook's hut. The bandit leader came out quickly. Bullet Head was right behind him. Meat Hook listened to the messenger, then he raised his hands and the mutants began to cheer.

"Father, father!" they chanted.

Before long the bandits turned and headed for Vinnie's dangling cage.

Miles peered into the dim twilight. "There it is."

Len looked over the windshield of the boat. He could see the northern tip of Lost Island. Miles gunned the throttle, throwing Len back in his seat, and the boat raced across the water.

"What are you doing?"

But Miles did not reply. He kept the boat on a southerly bearing, accelerating at top speed. He wanted to get to the southeastern end of the island. If Albright had indeed gone to the mutant camp, he would have to anchor the *Proteus* somewhere near the rock face in the natural harbor.

Len looked at the shape against the darkening sky. "You were right, Bookman."

The *Proteus* was anchored in the deep water off the rock face.

Miles steered toward the larger ship. "Let's see if we can get on board without getting ourselves killed."

Meat Hook and Bullet Head lowered Vinnie's cage, and Bullet Head tore open the door. Vinnie cowered against the bars of the cell.

Bullet Head grabbed his wrist and yanked him out of the cage. He dragged Vinnie toward Cannibal's caldron. Vinnie screamed, but Bullet Head dragged him past the bubbling stewpot.

Meat Hook pointed toward the altar. "The time of sacrifice is at hand. Take him on high!"

"Wait!" Vinnie cried.

A throng of bandits lifted him from the sand. They hoisted him aloft, carrying him to the altar. There they put him down, leaving two men to hold him. Vinnie's heart stopped when he saw a wide, curved silver blade coming at him in the torchlight.

"I don't see anyone," Len said.

Miles squinted in the purple darkness. "There are lights on in the control cabin. Maybe Albright is still here."

"Bookman, I'm not sure the doctor will be happy to see us. I mean, he did abandon us."

Miles sighed. "I don't think so. He probably

111

left us back at the other island because he didn't want us to get hurt while he tests his serum."

Len shook his head. "I don't know about this."

Miles put the boat in gear. "We've come this far. Let's do it."

He guided the boat up to the *Proteus*. Len reached up, grabbing the rail. When he had pulled himself over the side, Miles tossed a line up to him. Len secured the vessel, then helped Miles over the rail.

They hesitated for a moment, listening to the creaking of the ship.

"I don't hear anyone," Len said.

Miles pointed toward the control room. They went to the cabin, but the door seemed to be jammed. Pushing hard with their shoulders, they managed to get it open a couple of feet. Their faces went slack when they saw what had been blocking the door.

"A body," Len said. "Is it Albright?"

"No," Miles replied, "it's Stanley. He's dead." Tears began to form in Miles's eyes. "Hayden, Albright gave him that serum, just like me. That means—"

"No way!"

"I'm going to die, too," Miles said.

# Ten

The blade fell toward Vinnie's chest. They were going to cut out his heart. He screamed. He felt the tip of the sword against his chest. But the blade did not pierce his skin.

Vinnie couldn't believe what happened next. A man in a tuxedo leaped onto the platform. His face had been painted pink, and his dark hair had been slicked back with grease. He held a wireless microphone in his hand.

"Unbelievable," Vinnie muttered.

The man's clear voice came over speakers that had been mounted in the palm trees. "Welcome, my friends, to this week's episode of *The Wages of Sin,* Lost Island's number-one game show."

The bandits cheered like a studio audience.

The host gestured to mutants at the base of the platform. "What are the wages of sin?"

"Death!" the bandits replied in unison.

The host gestured toward Vinnie. "Now, let's meet our first contestant. He's originally from parts unknown, but he's been a guest on this island for quite some time. His name is Pelligrino, but Meat Hook has decided to give him a new name. Would you please give a rousing Lost Island welcome to the one, the only—Razorback!"

The mutants cheered Vinnie, chanting his new name.

"Razorback, huh?" the red-haired boy muttered.

The host gestured to the other end of the platform. "Our next contestant is from Apocalypse Island. He's a Ph.D., an M.D., and one all-around warped scientist. You know him as our lord and creator, the man who made us what we are. Please welcome Dr. Cyrus Albright!"

They booed as two men dragged an older man onto the stage. He was bald and wore a sweat-soaked linen suit. Vinnie heard him babbling about a serum that would make them all well again, but the bandits did not seem to be listening. They pushed Albright to his knees in front of Vinnie.

"Please," Albright shouted to them, "I can help you!"

The host grabbed the doctor's head and pulled it back. "We don't want any help, Father. We want to play *The Wages of Sin*!"

The bandits continued to boo.

Looking out over them, the host gave a hideous smile. "As you all know, the rules of the game are simple. One must die, one must live. Who do we want to die?"

"Father!"

"And who do we want to live?" the host asked.

"Razorback! Razorback!"

Vinnie chortled. "Razorback—that's me." He almost liked the sound of it.

The host put his hand on Vinnie's shoulder. "Do you hear that, Razorback? They want you to live!"

"I want to live," Vinnie replied.

The host looked out at the audience. "Do we want him to live? Is he our brother now!"

"Brother!"

"Razorback!"

The chanting rose to a feverish pitch. Vinnie felt something snap inside him. He could smell freedom. All he had to do was join in the game.

"Please," Albright said weakly, "listen to me—"

The host kicked Albright in the groin, and the doctor bent over. The host put his hand on Vinnie's shoulder again.

"Brother!"

"Razorback!"

The host went on, "Let's review the rules of

the game one more time. What are the rules of *Wages*?"

"One must die!"

"One must live!"

"One must die!"

"One must live!"

"That's right," the host replied, snapping his fingers. "May I have the sword please!"

Again the blade flashed in the twilight. The host took the weapon and waved it in the air. The mutants cheered even louder.

"Who do we want to live?"

"Razorback! Razorback!"

Music filtered in through the speakers. Sweat poured from Vinnie's face. He was ready to do anything to save his own life.

The host flashed his grin at the bandits. "Are you ready to play *The Wages of Sin*?"

"Death! Death!"

The host looked at Vinnie. "What about you, Razorback? Are you ready to go for the big jackpot?"

Vinnie nodded slowly.

"One must die!"

"One must live!"

"Razorback! Razorback!"

The host offered Vinnie the hilt of the sword. "Choose your weapon."

Vinnie grabbed the sword. He lifted the blade to look at the keen edge. The bandits went wild, pounding on the edge of the stage. Meat Hook and Bullet Head were right in front, cheering with the others.

"Now," the host said, "it wouldn't be right for one of us to kill our father. So we've chosen you for the task, Razorback. If you choose to play, to go for the jackpot, you'll be allowed to live."

Vinnie frowned. "You mean if I kill this old man, you won't kill me?"

"Not only will we not kill you, but you'll win an all-expense-paid trip to Lost Island! That's right, you'll be the guest of Meat Hook and his merry men. Why, he may even ask you to join his gang!"

"Razorback! Razorback!"

"What if I don't kill him?" Vinnie asked.

The host put his hand over his mouth for a moment. "You weren't listening. What are the wages of sin?"

"Death! Death!"

"If you choose not to play the game, you'll receive a consolation prize. One dirt-nap, compliments of Cannibal's caldron!"

"Dirt-nap! Dirt-nap!"

Vinnie lifted the sword in both hands. He did not have much choice—it was his life or the old man's.

Albright pleaded in front of him. "No, you must convince them to let me help. I have a serum. I can cure them."

"What say you, Razorback? Are you ready to play *The Wages of Sin*?"

Vinnie's eyes grew wider. "Sorry. It's you or me."

"Please—"

The host waved his hand. "Let the game begin!"

The mutants cheered as Vinnie raised the blade high over Albright's head.

Back on the *Proteus*, Miles was panicking. "I don't want to die, Hayden."

Len shook him. "Snap out of it, Bookman! You're not going to die."

"Yes I am," Miles said.

Len stared down at the body. "Maybe Albright had to kill him. Maybe he got out of control."

Miles shook his head. "The doctor would never have killed his patient. He would have taken him ashore to show the others they could be cured. No, he just died. The same thing is going to happen to me."

Len pushed past him, scanning the control station. "Look! The stun-gun." He went over to the keyboard and touched the weapon. "It hasn't been fired. Albright had it ready, but he didn't use it."

"That proves he didn't get out of hand. The serum killed him. It's going to kill me, Hayden."

Len looked at the keyboard. "The computer. Didn't Albright keep some kind of record for his experiments?"

Miles's eyes grew wide. "Yes, he transcribes notes from that book into the computer. I'll bring it up on the board."

Miles seemed to calm down as he took his place in the padded chair. His fingers began to move over the keyboard. Len gazed anxiously over Miles's shoulder.

"Hurry, Bookman!"

"It may take a while," Miles replied. "I have to crack the doctor's access code."

"There," Miles said. "I think I got it."

He had been working at the keyboard for over an hour. He had finally broken the doctor's password into the secret logs. Miles quickly moved to the entries made earlier that day.

"What does it say?" Len asked nervously.

Miles read directly from Albright's personal journal. "Here. 'Subject showing signs of weakness. Blood tests reveal toxins. Serum reacting with serum from previous experiments. Subject near death.' Man, the mutant passed on fast. But I'm still here."

"That's the answer!" Len cried. "You weren't injected with the first serum, so you won't have a reaction in your blood."

Miles leaned back, exhaling. "I'd already be

gone, if it killed the mutant so fast. Maybe I'm going to live after all."

"I wouldn't be so sure about that, punk!"

They turned quickly to look behind them. A bandit was standing at the rail. He held a crossbow on Len and Miles. When the bandit moved closer, Miles recognized him.

"Vinnie!"

Vinnie waved the crossbow at them. "I'm one of them now. You can call me Razorback. I joined up with Meat Hook. He trusts me now. He sent me here to look around."

Vinnie's arms were decorated with jagged red lines, like thunderbolts. The left side of his face was greased with red as well, and a small earring dangled from his right ear. His filthy pants were rolled up to his knees, exposing high black boots. Across the midsection of his T-shirt was scrawled the word *Razorback*.

Len shook his head. "I don't believe it."

"A person's got to stay alive," Vinnie replied. "Won't Meat Hook be surprised when I bring you back to the island?"

Miles looked quickly over Vinnie's shoulder. "Why don't you ask him now? He's right here. Hi, Meat Hook."

Vinnie wheeled to look behind him. "Huh?"

Miles reached for the stun-gun and fired the metal prongs into Vinnie's chest. Vinnie

**120**

twitched and fell unconscious to the floor of the cabin.

"Razorback," Miles said disgustedly. "Vinnie's as stupid as ever. Come on, let's get out of here. Albright wired this boat to blow up. I didn't want to tell you before."

Len gestured to the fallen boy.

"Leave him," Miles said. "C'mon, hurry."

They dived off the ship and pulled themselves over the side of the speed boat. Len untied the bow cleat and pushed them away. Miles pull-started the engine, which roared quickly to life.

Miles turned away from the *Proteus.* He gunned the outboard, and the boat roared away from the island. Len and Miles kept looking back, but saw no one.

"What now?" Len asked.

Miles pointed north. "Back to the island. Get some more gas from the compound and check out that hangar."

Len nodded. Miles held a steady course until the engine began to sputter. It finally died in the water.

"Out of gas," Miles said.

"Great," Len muttered. "Just great."

They floated across the open water, moving helplessly with the flow of the tide.

The sun broke the horizon in the east, casting a copper pallor on the deep blue water. A soft breeze blew in from the south, cooling the beach where Kirkland crouched in the sand. He was scanning the open sea with the binoculars that Albright had left behind in the lab, wondering why the mutants had not yet come to finish them.

Kirkland turned in a semicircle with the binoculars. He stopped dead when he saw a shape on the southern horizon, bobbing up and down in the choppy water.

"Cruiser, D.J.! Look!"

The other two boys were sleeping in the sand. They reluctantly came to life and moved beside Kirkland, looking to the south.

"What is it?" Cruiser asked.

"I don't know," Kirkland replied. "But it's coming this way."

"The mutants!" Cruiser said. "They're going to get us."

"No!" D.J. cried.

A southerly wind pushed the vessel toward the beach. It grew bigger in the binocular's lenses. Kirkland still didn't see anyone on the bobbing craft.

"It's a derelict," he said. "Abandoned."

"It has a motor," Cruiser said. "Let's grab it."

Kirkland and Cruiser swam to the vessel and pulled themselves over the side. They saw Len and Miles sleeping at opposite ends of the vessel.

"Wake up, preps!" Kirkland cried.

Len sat up slowly.

Miles opened his eyes and jumped up. "Kirkland!"

"Where'd you get the boat?" Cruiser demanded.

"That's not important," Miles replied. "We've got to make plans. There's a hangar on the other end of the island. You remember, Kirkland? I saw it when—"

Kirkland shook his head. "We're gonna take this boat and clear out of here. Let's get it into shore."

"You've got to listen," Miles went on. "The hangar is the safest place to be. The mutants will never—"

"Forget it, Bookman. We're outta here."

Miles sighed. "I'm telling you, we should try the hangar, Kirkland."

Kirkland pointed to the ocean. "Like I said, we're out of here."

Len and Miles exchanged a wary glance. Maybe it was better just to go along with them.

"At least take some food and water," Len said.

"We should be prepared," Miles offered.

Kirkland scowled at them. "Boy Scouts, huh? Okay, Hayden, you and Bookman are in charge of supplies. Go to it."

"We're going to need oil too," Miles replied. "That engine is a two stroke."

123

Cruiser frowned at them. "You're coming with us?"

Miles looked out over the blue water. "If we carry enough fuel and run slow, we might make it into a shipping lane. Of course, the hangar is probably—"

Kirkland gestured to the compound. "Go."

Miles looked straight at him. "Vinnie has joined Meat Hook and the other mutants. He's on their side now. We saw him on the *Proteus*."

"You're lying," Kirkland snapped. "Now go, or we'll leave without you."

Len and Miles didn't waste any time gathering the supplies. Still, it took them almost an hour to get back to the beach. They expected that the others would leave them, but Kirkland and crew were still there when Len and Miles emerged from the jungle.

Miles dropped his sack of supplies when he saw what lay beyond the beach. "Check it out, Hayden."

Len saw the *Proteus*. "Where did that come from?"

Kirkland and the others saw the boat as it drew closer to the island. Len and Miles ran down to the speed boat. The larger vessel was only a few hundred yards offshore.

Kirkland grabbed the oil and began to mix it in the gas tank. "We're taking the big boat now. Albright is going to answer to me."

**124**

"Albright is probably dead," Miles said coldy. "I don't like this, Kirkland. It's some kind of trick."

"Stay here then," Kirkland replied. "We're going home."

Kirkland launched the boat into the shorebreak. He pull-started the engine and headed straight for the *Proteus*.

As the speed boat approached the larger vessel, a figure appeared at the rail of the *Proteus*. Someone dived from the ship and began to swim toward them. Kirkland picked up a gas can to use as a weapon.

"No!" D.J. cried. "Look, it's Vinnie!"

Vinnie Pelligrino pulled himself over the side. He was dressed like the bandits from Lost Island. Red symbols were painted all over his body.

"Get this tub out of here," Vinnie said.

Kirkland frowned at his former friend. "What the—"

"Go!"

Vinnie grabbed the throttle and turned the steering wheel away from the *Proteus*. The boat had run only a hundred feet when the *Proteus* disappeared in a ball of flame. The explosion sent debris shooting in all directions.

Vinnie finally stopped the boat. Everyone had managed to cover up during the explosion—except D.J.

"He's dead!" Cruiser cried.

Vinnie lifted D.J.'s body and tossed it over the side.

Kirkland glared at Vinnie. "What happened to you?"

"I joined the winning team," Vinnie replied. "Meat Hook is all right. He sent me here to see if you guys want to join him. He respects you, Kirkland. He wants to make you one of his lieutenants."

Kirkland's eyes grew narrow. "Vinnie—"

"Razorback. That's my new name. Meat Hook will give you all new names."

Kirkland swung a hard right, knocking Vinnie out of the boat. Vinnie hit the water cursing. Kirkland quickly gunned the engine and took himself and Cruiser away from Razorback and the wreckage of the *Proteus*.

When the *Proteus* went up, Len and Miles hit the beach. Some debris landed around them, but they were unscathed by the blast. They both stood up as the smoke began to clear. Then they saw Kirkland driving north in the speed boat.

"That's the last we'll see of them," Len muttered.

Miles turned to look back at the mountains. "Let's head for the hangar. We can make it."

Len sighed.

Miles pointed to the bags of supplies that had

**126**

been forgotten. "We're ready—and we don't want to stay here."

Len looked to the south one more time. He could see someone swimming toward shore, and he also spotted sails on the horizon.

Len shivered. "You're right, Bookman. Let's go."

They traced the path back to the compound. After that, the mountain trail took them to the ledge that overlooked the south end of the island. In the recesses of the cave behind the ledge, Miles said the word *Proteus,* which opened a door in the rock wall.

A secret tunnel took them to the path that led down the other side of the mountain. By dusk, they were in the jungle. Miles built a fire, and they ate some of the food they had brought along.

They talked about the hangar. Miles had seen the huge white dome only once. An attack from the mutants had kept them from exploring it.

Suddenly they heard growling noises in the jungle. The pack of wild dogs had returned. Only this time, they did not have a flare gun to scare them off.

"Make torches!" Miles said. "We can fight them."

But they only managed to scatter the embers of the fire. The flames flickered and died. The leader of the pack came out to challenge them.

Miles groped for a weapon, but something rushed over him, springing into the night. They heard dogs fighting in the darkness.

Len felt a hand against his back. "Augie!"

The smaller boy had emerged from the shadows. He looked anxiously toward the sound of the dog fight. He had to save his friends, but he was afraid for Commando.

There was a final yelp. Len held his breath. Augie bolted into the darkness. Len and Miles called after him, but he didn't stop.

Augie's voice finally echoed through the jungle. "It's okay."

They moved toward the sound of the boy's voice. They found Augie with the pack curled around him. The wild dog leader was dead. The pack now followed Augie and Commando.

"Come with us," Miles said.

Augie shook his head. "I belong here. Nobody hurts me here."

"Please, Augie," Len said.

But Augie had already started away from them. He disappeared in the jungle with the dogs at his heels.

Miles whistled. "We've seen some stuff, Hayden."

Len sighed. "We've seen too much."

They couldn't sleep, so they decided to move on. The flat desert lay ahead after the jungle. It

**128**

was the quickest way to reach the mountains where Miles had seen the hangar. And they could make much better time in the coolness of the night.

# Eleven

"Sir Charles?"

The tall Englishman turned toward the clerk at the hotel desk. "Yes, I'm Sir Charles Bookman."

The clerk held out a large envelope. "This came for you while you were out."

Sir Charles took the envelope from the clerk's hand. "Thank you."

Sitting quickly on a sofa in the hotel lobby, he ripped open the envelope. There was no postmark—Colgan had been using private couriers.

His eyes scanned the page. "Blast! No luck at all."

Colgan had found no trace of the wrecked plane so far. Sir Charles wadded up the message. He was tired of waiting.

He would give Colgan one more week, then begin his appeal to higher authorities. Miles would be found sooner or later. Sir Charles just hoped he would be found alive.

"Come on, Hayden. You can do it!"

Miles extended his hand to Len, who hesitated on the rock face. They were almost to the top of the mountain. The climb had been exhausting.

"Gut it out," Miles said.

"Give me a minute to rest. That doctor didn't inject me with any serum."

Miles lifted his eyes to the south. They had crossed the desert without any trouble. The springs at the base of the mountains had been a welcome sight.

The climb had gone well until now. Miles looked over his shoulder. The summit was just above them. They could not stop now.

"Hayden!"

"All right, all right!"

Len grunted as he fought his way to the ledge. Miles reached down to grab his wrist and pulled Len over the crag.

"We're almost there," Miles said. "Just a little more."

Len glanced up at the peak. "That's it?"

Miles nodded. "Give me a lift up."

Len boosted him to the rim of the ledge. Miles ascended, then stood up and made a whistling noise.

"What do you see?" Len asked.

Miles turned back to lower his hand. "Come up and have a look for yourself."

Len fought his way over the final obstacle. He stood next to Miles and peered down into the spectacular green valley. He saw the large white dome that rested between the mountains.

"The hangar," Miles said proudly.

"It's huge!" Len replied.

Miles turned, taking in the scenery. This was once a beautiful place.

Then he saw the ocean. "Hayden!"

"What?"

"On the water."

Len turned pale. "Not again."

Meat Hook's fleet had already set up camp on the beach. Their boats were everywhere. When Miles squinted toward the hangar, he could see the tiny mutants, winding around the perimeter of the large white dome.

Branch Colgan studied the fuel gauge of the C-47. He was getting close to a crucial point in his navigation. He had used almost half his fuel, which meant he either had to turn back or find a place ahead of him to refuel the plane.

He looked at his charts. He had never been so far south. There was nothing on the map, but he knew he was in Omega quadrant.

Colgan made a hasty decision. He would push on beyond the halfway mark. He felt as if he were close to something. If he had to ditch, he could send out a mayday before he went down. The plane was equipped with a life raft and emergency supplies.

Colgan sweated as the red needle dropped closer to empty. He kept the plane steady over the wide blue water. His heart had begun to pound.

"It's got to be here!"

He was almost out of fuel, but his eyes continued to study the far horizon. He finally saw a speck in the distance. It rose out of the sea, growing larger as he drew closer to the land mass.

The right engine began to sputter. Colgan headed for the island. He spotted a small level area, covered with shrubs and tall grass. He hoped he could find a big enough clearing to land!

*Will the boys escape at last, or will their last hope of rescue be forever dashed? Find out in Escape from Lost Island #4,* **Discovered!**

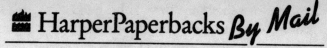

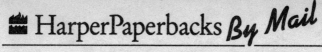